# The
# Floating City

Also by Pamela Ball

*Lava*

# The Floating City

A NOVEL

## Pamela Ball

Pamela Ball
Tallahassee, Florida
March, 2002

Viking

VIKING
Published by the Penguin Group
Penguin Putnam Inc., 375 Hudson Street, New York, New York 10014, U.S.A.
Penguin Books Ltd, 80 Strand, London WC2R 0RL, England
Penguin Books Australia Ltd, 250 Camberwell Road, Camberwell,
Victoria 3124, Australia
Penguin Books Canada Ltd, 10 Alcorn Avenue, Toronto, Ontario, Canada M4V 3B2
Penguin Books (N.Z.) Ltd, Cnr Rosedale and Airborne Roads, Albany,
Auckland, New Zealand

Penguin Books Ltd, Registered Offices: Harmondsworth, Middlesex, England

First published in 2002 by Viking Penguin, a member of Penguin Putnam Inc.

1   3   5   7   9   10   8   6   4   2

LIBRARY OF CONGRESS CATALOGING IN PUBLICATION DATA
Ball, Pamela.
The floating city / Pamela Ball.
p.   cm.
ISBN 0-670-89472-9
1. Hawaii—History—1893–1900—Fiction.   2. Norwegians—Hawaii—Fiction.
3. Honolulu (Hawaii)—Fiction.   4. Fortune tellers—Fiction.   I. Title.
PS3552.A4554 F58 2002
813'.54—dc21        2001026805

This book is printed on acid-free paper. ∞

Printed in the United States of America
Set in Cochin
Designed by Nancy Resnick

*For Claire Hanson Ball*

*And For Gary White*

# *Acknowledgments*

For steering me in the right direction during the writing of this book, I'd especially like to thank four invaluable friends: Lu Vickers, Pat MacEnulty, Steve Watkins, and the late Jerry Stern, whose advice and encouragement are always with me. My thanks also go to Lisa Munroe and the glop porch, Stuart Riordan, Bucky McMahon, Kim Garcia, and Pete Ripley. I'd also like to thank Georgia Vail and Taylor Erwin for their wild optimism, and Cynthia Hollis for navigation. For seeing the manuscript through, I'd like to thank Carole DeSanti and Karen Murphy. Lastly, I'd like to thank Connie May Fowler and Joy Harris, for making it possible in the first place.

# The Floating City

# Prologue

The dead man's journey began above Honolulu, in one of the teahouses that orbit the city like hidden satellites. Behind the teahouse was Nuuanu Stream, which carried the dead man past houses tucked away behind a bamboo forest, past a Buddhist nun pulling a bucket of morning water from the stream, a nun who treated him like a secret, setting down her bucket to silently watch him pass by. He floated between the rich houses of the missionaries, houses solidly built against Northern winters, as if they had brought their cold weather with them, as well as their cold religion. Then past the ephemeral mansions of the sugar barons, which were always painted white, topped with cupolas that twisted like spun sugar, where a lonely woman in a white dress waited on an upper balcony, a woman who had married sugar, and was now drowning under the weight of it. Farther downstream, he floated past the mausoleum of the Hawaiian royalty, a small building that held the Hawaiian dead under a steep roof, and then he glided between the houses of merchants, where the stream narrowed. In the shallows, the dead man waited for rain, for the stream to swell up higher than the rocks he was caught on, and then moved down through the modest neighborhoods crowded with the sounds of cockfights, love affairs, street vendors calling their wares in voices sharp as insects, ukuleles tuned slack and played loud to drown out the dire forecasts of the streetcorner missionary who warned that hell was even hotter than Honolulu. He drifted past women dark as shadows who kissed sailors from the other side of the world, while old men smoked opium and listened to the cocks crow and the churchbells answer.

The curve of the stream was crowded with the sounds of hula classes and dance halls, birds calling across the narrowing stream now used as a rubbish dump, where he hid for hours under the weeds and garbage, until the rain forced him closer to Honolulu Harbor. He passed a banana patch and a group of small boys fishing who ran home and told of seeing a dead man with thick dark hair, but no one believed them. The boys almost didn't believe themselves, and they listened to what their parents said, that they'd seen the ghost of a dead ancestor, and they were glad that even in the afterlife you could keep your thick black hair. The dead man glided past the noisy sailors' bars in downtown Honolulu, the tattoo parlors where young men pledged their love across nervous skin, and past the empty temperance houses and the full brothels, where the women hung their muumuus over the railings like brightly colored flowers. Through the opening of the stream the dead man rode the muddy water fanning across Honolulu Harbor, bumping against the pilings of the pier until a storm pulled him past the sampans, rowboats, and an American warship the size of a luxury hotel, and the tide sent him into a small, rocky cove.

*An island rises out of the sea and the trouble begins. So it always goes.*

*When Kamehameha the Great pulled all of the Hawaiian Islands into his fist, for the first time there was one king, one rule, one country. And then, when the foreign ships arrived with their sails the color of death, the people wondered if this was a curse upon them, to be visited by such an apparition. Soon, boats from more countries than they'd known existed filled the bays, and other harbors were found to hold what the world was sending their way.*

*Kamehameha died in 1819, and the following year, the missionaries arrived, and nothing was ever the same.*

# One

$\mathcal{H}$onolulu is a place that reminds you of what you are not. Eva was not Hawaiian. She was not American. She was not a wife or a mother. She was clairvoyant, but her talent was like an untrained dog; it came when it wanted to, not because it was called.

The palms whispered overhead, and the early morning sky above Honolulu was a pink as soft as the inside of a baby's mouth, and perhaps that was all anyone could be certain of. As Eva and Lehua rode their bicycles towards the cove, Eva kept counting the things she was not. The age on her identification card was several years older than her actual age of twenty-five. The name on her identification card wasn't her own name. In Honolulu, her name was Eva Hanson.

With their long skirts tucked up around their legs, they glided down watery roads still wet with dew, as if skimming over the surface of a river. Heading downhill, their wheels sent out sprays of water as thin as the blade of a knife, as bright as a prayer. They lived at the very top of the hill, in an old house that leaned makai, towards the sea.

Across the street from their home was the orphanage for Hawaiian girls. Lehua herself had grown up in the same large house, which had been built for the children of lepers. An orphanage for children who were not quite orphans.

Now Lehua taught them how to dance hula, and Eva told their fortunes and showed them how to play poker. The most important thing in life was to know what was worth counting, but they already understood this. The old sailors who lived next door told the children stories of whales that stayed up at the surface of the water for so long that trees and plants grew on their backs. Ships moored next to the whales, and unsuspecting sailors stepped out of their boats, thinking they were on dry land.

The old men stomped their feet on the ground, winked, said, "Sure, it feels like soil, but who knows?" The girls drew a collective breath and let it out slowly. Eva once found them furtively digging with a shovel in the backyard of the orphanage, not digging to reach the other side of the world, not to China, but to reach the back of the whale. Who knows? In this country, nothing was as it appeared. A field of lava collapsed into the sea faster than a love affair ended.


*T*here were two things they didn't speak of when they went fishing: the dead and the living. Instead, they talked about bamboo, the liquid sound of it, how in a grove of bamboo you could shut your eyes and hear the deep hollow sound of the ocean. How there was nothing luckier than a bamboo fishing pole already carrying this sound in it.

Then they cheated a little and talked about the Chinese women around them, on a rare day free from fieldwork, women with beautiful thin arms, and eyes like drops of water. They dove into the sea and emerged with their clothing tight against their slender bodies like a caul, like a breath pulled inward.

As the end of the nineteenth century approached, the dead had become as restless as the living. But Eva and Lehua didn't talk of the dead. They fished in water up to their waists, felt the push of waves against their bodies, and waited for uama, the small fish that ran like clouds of silver under the surface of the water. And they didn't speak of Queen Lili'uokalani, whose monarchy had been overthrown two years earlier, in 1893. They didn't speak of the rumors that Royalists loyal to the Queen were on the verge of attacking the new Republic. Events were building even at that moment, as they cast their lines into water shared with an American warship.

They didn't speak of this. They were fishing.

The Chinese women flicked their fishing poles quick as riding crops over the surface of the water, each of them fishing in a different manner, in ways that they were certain brought them luck.

There was a silence when the fish were present, a low murmur of voices when there were no fish.

Eva kept an eye on Lehua, the way she was fishing and yet not fishing, which meant that she was thinking of her husband. Just before he died of the smallpox brought in by the foreign ships, he wrapped the handle of her fishing pole in string so fine that a single strand of it would disappear. A handle the colors of an uhu, the lucky colors of a parrot fish.

Like so many others in Honolulu, Lehua was secretive and sometimes disappeared for days on end. At first, Eva hoped that Lehua's occasional absences were due to a lover, but she soon found out it was opium.

Now, when Lehua disappeared, Eva and their neighbor Tomas went downtown to the small wooden buildings that housed the opium dens. Inside, the rooms looked like a shipwreck, the sleeping pallets stacked up like shelves, and the people curled up on them were like crumpled belongings, something too valuable to throw away and yet too damaged to use. When they found her, Lehua was not surprised to see them. Nothing surprised her. Even awake it seemed she was sleepwalking, glassy-eyed, her long hair tangled down her back like a bad dream slowly becoming visible. The first time Eva saw

*The Floating City* · 7

Lehua in that state, she had wept at the hand Lehua had been dealt. And yet weeping over another person's sadness was like watching a house burn down and doing nothing to put the fire out, to save what could be saved.

Lehua was nearly as tall as Eva but much thinner, her bones visible beneath the skin. Her body was easy to carry, with that odd heavy lightness of a sleeping child.


*T*oday the fish were small and came in wild circles. The women waded farther out, towards the rocks at the mouth of the bay, and the fish scattered in every direction and a moment later clustered and swam off.

As Eva caught a fish, she quickly took it off the hook and placed it in the woven bag tied to her body. When there were enough fish, the bag lifted up and swam in its own direction, tugging gently against her waist.

Today the fishing was slow and Lehua told her a story about her mother, which did not break their living or dead rule, because officially Lehua was an orphan. Unofficially, her mother still lived on the island of Molokai, at the crowded leper colony.

Lehua's mother once caught a fish that was kapu, off limits for commoners. She was fishing along a deserted part of the shoreline which was kapu as well, a place meant only for the ali'i, for royalty. She would have been punished with death for eating this rare fish, but there was a terrible famine and she was pregnant with Lehua and so she ate the fish meant for chiefs. And as she ate, she pretended for a moment that she herself was Queen, not just of Oahu, but of all the Hawaiian Islands. When her mother finished eating, her kingdom shrank back down to the size of her opu, Lehua said, patting her stomach.

"I wonder what it tasted like?" Eva asked, trying to imagine a flavor so fine it was saved for royalty.

"Oh, Eva," Lehua said, rolling her eyes, "tasted like fish."

*A* story often told about Kamehameha the Great was that one day he was talking to a Christian sailor and the man claimed that his Christian God was more powerful than all the Hawaiian Gods put together.

Kamehameha thought about this for a moment, then suggested as proof that the Christian man should jump from a cliff and Kamehameha himself would see whether or not his powerful Christian God would save him.

# $\mathcal{T}wo$

$\mathcal{A}$ young girl ran down the beach towards them, running the way people did when they were being chased, her panic visible, her black hair a dark wing flying behind her. No one understood what she was yelling and her mother said something back in Mandarin Chinese and the women frowned and clacked their tongues against the roofs of their mouths, a sound of disapproval. Everyone tried to keep the children speaking the language of their own race, but most of them spoke pidgin, a combination of languages that was mainly English. People speak it, Lehua said, but they don't have to like it. She said English was an iron bit in your mouth.

The girl gestured excitedly, pointing out towards the crumbling rocks. Her mother quickly scooped up a handful of water and threw it like spit, to keep the bad luck away.

Eva heard enough to know that the girl had found a drowned man in the curve of the bay. She ran her fingers nervously through her net bag, grabbed hold of a small uama, and held it tight in her fist, felt the tail flicking against her palm like a heartbeat.

The women hurried along the edge of the water, climbed over

the rocks to help lift the body and bring it up on the beach, above the high tide line. As soon as they turned him over, Eva wished they hadn't. Now he wasn't simply a body. He had a face, he mattered. His hair was black, but he'd been in the water too long and his features were hidden, as if even his bones had softened.

Eva felt a panic, a sense that she was to blame. Ridiculous, she told herself, opening her eyes. She'd never seen him before. His death had nothing to do with her.

He wore a shirt made of raw silk, and expensive trousers. There was a rope burn around his neck. Lehua believed he was murdered by the Americans, and the Chinese women agreed with her. "Venereal disease and smallpox and measles are too slow," she said bitterly, "so now they are strangling us."

Eva put a scarf over his face, so Lehua wouldn't think of her dead husband, then quickly went through his pockets for identification. It was important to remove everything before the police arrived. She knew what the police did with information they found, used it to hound the living.

His pockets were empty.

Eva couldn't help herself. When no one was watching, she picked up his hand and turned it over, looking for the lines on his palm that brought him here, but his hand was wrinkled by the sea and unreadable. She ran her finger across his skin, and as she set his hand back down, she noticed a bit of green the color of seaweed clinging to his cuff. She pulled the sleeve back. A jade necklace on a silk cord was wound tight around his wrist. She turned his arm over and found the clasp to unhook the cord, which had left a deep indentation in his flesh.

The jade flashed bright green in Eva's hand, jade the color of a rare tree frog, the color of American money. No one around her seemed to be watching, so she slipped the jade into her pocket and joined the group still trying to comfort the young girl.

The girl was struggling so hard not to cry that she was hic-cupping. Eva gave the girl her bag of fish, because it would be good for the child to have something to carry, and a job to do when she got home.

The police needed to be told about the dead man, but no one was willing to volunteer. The immigration laws had tightened against Asians. Once they were seen as cheap and needed labor, but as their numbers in Hawaii increased, the Americans had coined the term yellow peril, and took legal steps to control the number of immigrants who weren't white. The women would be in trouble simply for being Chinese, never mind finding a body. Indentured workers' contracts could be sold to anyone with enough money, and no one cared if it broke up a family.

Lehua had watched her take the jade, and now she gave Eva a look that said the least she could do was inform the police her-self.

Eva resisted. Who in her right mind would voluntarily go to the police? Her business was fortunetelling with a bit of petty larceny on the side, nothing she wanted closely examined. She glanced at the worried faces around her. To them, Eva was the only choice. She was haole, white skinned, a color the police wouldn't be suspicious of.

"Eva," Lehua said, holding out her hand.

Eva couldn't bear the thought of giving up the jade. "All right," she finally said, "I'll go."

Lehua turned to the group and explained that the haole woman would take care of everything.

Eva was surrounded by smiling women who suddenly thought of her as a hero, when actually she was simply the new owner of an expensive piece of jade, which she planned to hock as soon as possible.

Out of respect for the dead, an older woman offered to stay a moment with the drowned man. She loosened her gray hair, which fell almost to her waist, and then braided it again, her old hands moving quick as a girl's. She smoothed the wrinkles from her clothes and squatted down in the sand next to the body.

Lehua and Eva rode back through the sugar cane fields, balancing their poles and fishing gear across the handlebars of their bicycles. From far away, cane fields looked like a soft green sea, but up close the leaves cut like knives. The women who worked in the fields wrapped themselves in thick clothing to protect their skin and they looked like ghosts moving through the sharp blades of the cane.

In the firebreak the dirt was almost too soft, like pedaling through ash. It sifted over them in a fine red layer, and even Lehua's brown hair turned ehu, dusted in red. Eva thought they looked like circus clowns.

Lehua said no, they were the color of warriors. Her bicycle wobbled through the soft dirt. "It could be a political murder," she warned. "He could be a Royalist."

"Perhaps he drowned, nothing more than that," Eva answered, but she was thinking of the rope burns around his neck.

As she pedaled through the dirt, Eva thought how at first the dead man did not look like anything at all, just a body washed in from the sea. Now, she thought, he looks like all of us.

*I*n New England in October 1819, there were signs that the Second Coming of Christ was imminent. People fell ill from strange ailments, their tongues thickened in their mouths, forcing them to speak with gestures. Clouds of birds blocked the sun, and under that shadow six bachelor missionaries made a hasty search for wives.

How easy is it to find a bride at a moment's notice? Perhaps it depends on where the search takes place. So much of our lives is defined by geography.

Less than a month later, armed with new brides and Bibles, they left Boston for Hawaii, a journey of eighteen thousand miles and 159 days.

What sort of women were these, who would marry complete strangers, then embark on such a long journey in a small boat crammed with Calvinists, chickens, pigs, supplies, freshly inscribed Bibles linking their names with their husbands'? The young women did their growing up quickly, in the dark rocking hull of a boat the width of three brooms laid end to end.

Sheets were hung between the narrow cots to promote the illusion of privacy, and the nausea of seasickness was quickly followed by the nausea of pregnancy.

# Three

$\mathcal{A}$t the beach cove, the dead man was discovered by several fishermen who squatted around him in a worried circle. Was this a good death or a bad death? One of the men unbuttoned the dead man's shirt and, when he saw the rope mark burnt into the man's neck, joked that a good death is the one that happens to someone else.

No one laughed.

Hands brushed the sand from his body, fingers combed the wet hair back off his face, squeezed the salt water from his clothes. He looked more asleep than dead, his flesh oddly firm, his color rich. They carried him under the thorny kiawe trees that grew along the edge of the cove, and the shadows of branches waved like seaweed across his face.

They lifted him into the back of a wagon and began the journey back to Honolulu. Along the way they argued whether to take him to the police, who would file his death and promptly forget about him, or to take him to someone who might be able to find out why he was murdered.

Along the rocky coast of crumbling a'a lava, they passed other fishermen who stood with one foot propped, storklike, men who barely glanced at the cart, their eyes on the water, their throw nets draped over one shoulder like a cloak.

The wagon dipped down into the fields of sugar cane that were once sandalwood forests and across irrigation ditches that were once streams full of opai, all of it now owned by foreigners, and all of it given over to sugar. Not long ago there were only a few sugar cane plantations, but within several years there were over sixty, and it took hours to get through the green sea of cane that grew all the way to the edges of the cliffs.

The cane fields gave way to banana and papaya farms. Here, the grass was longer and the horse slowed its pace and the white pipi birds lifted and settled, escorting the wagon.

Skirting the edge of a waterfall, the road became softer and the men climbed down from the wagon and pushed from behind, their legs calf-high in mud.

The cart passed Honolulu Harbor, where several years ago small red fish ran like blood under the pier when King Kalakaua announced his upcoming trip to the United States. When the King's ship returned draped in funeral bunting, people remembered the red fish and they were not surprised by his death. Stricken, but not surprised.

Today there were no red fish in the clear water. Yet who needed a sign of bad luck when there was a warship full of American Marines just offshore?

The streets were swarming with vegetable vendors who steered their bicycles with one hand and balanced heavy baskets of produce with the other. Messengers on black bicycles darted past the tired horse, light as insects on the surface of the water.

They were stopped by a patrol of soldiers. The fishermen stood nervously watching the soldiers poke through the pile of fishing gear they'd used to cover the body.

"What's this?" a young soldier asked excitedly, lifting the edge of a net. He glanced around for an answer, but the fishermen had scattered.

It was too big a surprise for them to bother pursuing the men who ran away. They'd been ordered to keep an eye out for the body of one man in particular, and told that if they found him there would be a reward. Under no circumstances was the body to be taken to the police.

Perhaps this was the man. The young soldier stared down at the feet of the dead man, wondering if all dead people had such vulnerable looking feet.

The cart was pulled under a large 'ulu tree that grew at the end of a small dirt path. Above them, an old man who had climbed the tree to hanai a few breadfruit held his body perfectly still. It wasn't his tree and he didn't want trouble over stealing breadfruit.

He had cut one fruit, and the milky sap dripped onto the ground, but no one noticed. He shifted his weight and calculated how many hours his cramped legs could last in a tree. Perhaps it was best for a dead man to be brought under such a tree as an 'ulu, the old man thought. Breadfruit was favored by the gods, and useful as well.

The soldiers decided to go back to their headquarters to find out where to take the body, and after they left the old man slowly slid down the thick trunk of the 'ulu tree, the pain in his bad leg biting like a dog. He placed a round green 'ulu in the dead man's hand and limped off into the shadows.

*Under pressure from the missionaries, King Liholiho abolished the old kapu system, a complicated structure of taboos that defined the daily life of the Hawaiian people.*

*The missionaries quickly replaced the King's kapu system with one of their own, called the Ten Commandments.*

*Old Hawaiian beliefs became porous as coral. Doubt set in. Even the language could no longer be trusted. For example, the Hawaiian word for adultery was moe kolohe. Sleeping mischievously. A term used without malice until the arrival of the missionaries, who informed the Hawaiians that it was kapu.*

*Under the new kapu system, there would be no dancing of hula, no wearing of flower leis, no cooking fires on the Sabbath, no horseback riding. No moe kolohe.*

# Four

$E$va and Lehua parted ways under the banyan tree that stretched across several streets in the center of Honolulu. Everything that moved came for shade under that tree, workers eating lunch, scraggly roosters keeping themselves just out of reach of panting dogs, lei sellers protecting their flowers from the sun, small children playing, children who were old enough to be in school.

"Meet me later, Eva. There's a rally this afternoon, in support of the Queen. Come hear the speeches."

Eva shook her head. This was not her struggle, and it was best to steer clear of it. Going to the police was enough trouble for one day.

"Good luck," she said, as she turned her bicycle downhill, her feet held out to the sides, pedals churning wildly. Luck, she wondered, do I believe in it myself?

When she turned onto Beretania it took a moment to realize that the street was empty. Closed signs hung in shop windows. An abandoned water wagon sat at the side of the road, the horse sleeping in the hot sun. The fruit stands were empty, and so was the trolley when it passed by. Everyone was gathered at the harbor.

She set her bicycle against the wall of the jail. As she pushed opened the door, she felt her body shrinking. It's not as if the building itself is poison, she scolded herself.

The room was empty except for two policemen engaged in a serious discussion. One of them glanced up, registered her presence, then turned back to his conversation.

"It's not possible," he said, mopping his face with his sleeve. His dark eyes were set too far apart, giving him the look of a startled horse.

"But it's true," the other answered, shaking his head. "This town," he muttered, and then looked up at Eva.

"May I help you?" he suddenly asked in a voice that promised the opposite.

A moment earlier she could have fled, lied to Lehua that she had gone to the police station and given her information, and that would have been the end of it.

She began nervously explaining about the dead man who washed into the bay. "He had a rope burn around his neck. He'd been strangled."

They looked at her suspiciously. One of them left the room and the other one continued to stare at her.

"Strangled, you say."

Perhaps it was wrong to be so specific. "I could have been mistaken," she said quickly.

They exchanged a glance.

"Yet there were marks on the skin?"

"Ah. I can't really be certain. The shock of it . . ."

The policeman held his hand up to stop her. "Enough talking," he said excitedly.

"Enough?"

"Write it down." He handed her a piece of paper and a bottle of ink with the cap nearly rusted shut. Eva noticed a tattoo on the back of his wrist that she guessed to be a frog, though she couldn't be certain. In Honolulu, it was a common practice to fill a man up with liquor and then throw him at the mercy of a tattoo artist, though it was a fate usually reserved for sailors rather than policemen.

The paper was damp where his hands had touched it, and the ink wavered as she wrote. On the lower half of the page she drew a small map of the cove and hesitated a moment before placing an x where they'd left the body.

*I pulled the man up above the high tide line,* she wrote, as if he was something she'd salvaged from the sea.

She felt a sudden connection to him, something flowing between them that was gone before she could grasp hold of it, but the strange feeling remained. Perhaps he had been as ill at ease in a police station as she was, she told herself. Perhaps it was nothing more than that.

The policeman took the paper from her and told her to wait. A door opened in the back of the station, and he put his finger to his lips and leaned forward, straining to hear. Rough voices carried down the hall towards them. Eva couldn't understand what was being said, just that the tone was threatening.

The door slammed shut and it was quiet in the room.

"What is it?" she asked.

"Nothing. Nothing at all." He left the room and returned with another policeman, who was far more excited, his face the bright pink color of the inside of a guava.

"Who do you think this dead person was?"

It was a dangerous question. They wanted to know if she recognized him as a Royalist, as someone in favor of reinstating the monarchy. Yet, if there was a possibility of a reward, she wanted to be certain that she received it. It made Eva cautious. "Perhaps he was a laborer," she said carefully.

The policeman slapped the desk with his wet palm and announced that the three of them would go down to the beach to retrieve the body and bring it back to town.

Eva said she couldn't possibly do that, she was far too busy.

The policeman raised his eyebrows. "We are not asking, Miss Hanson. This is a police matter. And I think you have more than enough free time. Time enough to fish, eh?" he added.

He stood up, motioning her to the door. A moment later she found herself crowded into a rickety black cart, with a small sign declaring it to be property of the Honolulu Police Department. Her hands were suddenly wet, her face damp in the heat.

They rode through Honolulu and then headed into the cane fields. Eva reached into her pocket and fingered the jade that had put her here, squeezed between two policemen. She wondered how much money she'd receive for it, and whether the jade was worth going through this much trouble. And yet, if she had left it tied around the man's wrist, someone else would have stolen it by now, and that would never do.

A Chinese herbalist in downtown Honolulu had told her that when a person was buried with a piece of jade placed on his chest the jade would change color as the body decomposed, and so it was thought to be a living stone. Her jade was still bright as new cane.

When they reached the beach, Eva took the policemen down to the cove and they hiked across the sand to the place where she had left the body.

The beach was empty except for a few pieces of driftwood. Above the high tide line, the sand ran into a cluster of thorny kiawe trees. Eva licked her lips, felt her palms dampen. Where was the body? Was someone else claiming the reward? She scooped up a handful of dry sand, let it trickle between her fingers. "Right here. I left him right here."

She pulled her jacket tighter around her. A fever, she decided, I must be coming down with a fever.

"Are you sure you haven't imagined this, Miss Hanson?" the tall policeman asked. "Tropical heat often causes young women, especially a fair redhead such as yourself, to imagine something that isn't there."

She shook her head. "I did not imagine him."

He looked at her suspiciously. "Perhaps your sense of geography is pilau, eh? Maybe all these bays look alike to you? Just rocks, sand, kiawe trees?"

"I dragged him here," Eva insisted, "above the water line."

"Well, there are no tracks." He looked up and down the beach, then turned to her, holding his arms open. "You predict the future, don't you?" he asked. "Tell us what happened."

She gave him a look that she hoped withered his soul. "Disappearing bodies are not my specialty."

The policeman's startled eyes settled on her a moment, then veered off.

"This is a serious matter, Miss Hanson."

"No doubt."

He looked from the water's edge to where they stood. "How was it possible for you to drag the body such a distance?"

Meaning, *who was with you,* she thought.

She stood up and rolled her sleeve above the elbow. She stuck her arm out to the side and flexed her muscle. She was tall and thin, but as strong as most men her size.

They glanced at each other. From somewhere a dog barked, and the taller policeman took off his hat. He sat down in the sand, fanning himself. A slight breeze wrinkled the water offshore, but around them the air was hot and still, and sweat trickled down his face.

The tattooed policeman started talking. "You know, a whole beach can disappear in one storm. But I always wonder, where does that sand go? It has to go someplace."

The other policeman sighed and shook his head. "So you walk one way," he said, pointing his hat at Eva. He turned to the other policeman. "And you walk the other way, try find a body. Try find anything, missing sand even. And I will sit here and wait."

He closed his eyes. "So go," he said, his thick hand motioning them away.

Eva nervously searched along the high tide line. Whoever moved the body hadn't taken it to the police. Why was that? And where would they have taken it?

She closed her eyes, trying to see what had occurred. At first there was nothing. Then black canvas shoes, the kind that fishermen wore to walk across the reef. A thin palm frond swept over the sand to erase footprints.

When she opened her eyes, the policemen were standing together, watching her carefully.

She shook the sand from her skirt. "Perhaps it was another bay after all," she said. "Or it could be that the body washed back out to sea."

"That would take a storm, Miss Hanson, and there have been no storms."

They rode back to Honolulu without speaking. The horse moved slowly in the thick heat, and the man holding the reins slept through the cane fields, his chin wobbling with the motions of the cart. His hands were plump, and the tattooed frog rested there as if in a pond of muddy water.

Eva decided that if there were further questions she'd agree she'd imagined it all, anything to sever this connection to the police.

Outside the jail in Honolulu, soldiers circled a crowd of angry people. The soldiers had broken up the group gathered down at the harbor, preventing the Royalists from speaking on behalf of the Queen.

A man grabbed hold of the reins of the police cart, and Eva and the policemen were pulled to the ground. As she scrambled to her feet, a distraught woman took hold of her arm, then grabbed a handful of Eva's hair and pulled her close. She smelled of rum. "Eh, what happens next? You kilokilo, right?"

"Yes," Eva agreed, she was the fortuneteller, but how could anyone know what would happen next?

They were carried with the crowd. Eva struggled to keep her footing, and the woman leaned against her, still holding onto her hair.

A man pulled the boards off the side of the cart. The seat cushions had already been stolen.

Eva's neighbor Tomas was in the crowd, a man too old and frail to be out in a pushing mob. Eva pulled loose from the woman and made her way over to him.

"Ah, Eva," he yelled, holding up his walking stick. "I've a notion to use this on one of those soldiers." He shook his cane at a soldier, who slapped it from his hand. Eva scrambled to retrieve it. "Come on," she said, "let's get you out of here."

A soldier picked up Eva's bicycle and swung it around him in circles, forcing the crowd to back away from the jail.

"Pupule," the man next to her said, making a circle around his ear to signify crazy. The woman with him was crying.

The soldier was now using the bicycle like a pitchfork, pushing it into the retreating crowd. He smashed it down on the sidewalk until the front wheel was knocked loose from the frame.

Eva had seen the soldier's gesture before, on the day her father took her to see the lions. Lions in Norway. They walked across puddles of ice to the tent of the traveling zoo. She held her father's hand and the ice cracked underfoot and it sounded like the bones in his hand were breaking. Her father wanted her to enjoy the lions, to show some childhood fear or excitement, but she couldn't muster it. The tent was freezing, the lions roared, and the lion tamer swung a chair to keep the animals away from him. Her father took off his wool scarf and wrapped it around Eva's neck. She thought the lions roared because they were so cold, because they knew they were in the wrong place, in the wrong country. Watching the lion tamer, she realized how off kilter the world was. Nothing she'd seen since then had made her change her mind.

On the way home, Tomas forgot the street they lived on, and Eva gently turned him in the right direction. His memory was a sea he fished across every day. Dropped a line, and waited. Eva never knew what he'd pull up. Some days, nothing. Other days, a harvest of the past.

"I should have been braver, Eva."

"What are you saying? You were very brave."

"No. But truth is, I don't like jail. My heart is too old for confinement," he said, tapping his concave chest.

At the end of the street, there were lanterns swinging in the dark. Eva pulled Tomas to the side of the road as they waited for the soldiers to pass by, the swinging light causing their shapes to waver like snakes before they disappeared.

*K*ing Liholiho's curiosity about the world could no longer be con-
tained. He chose to visit England. The American missionaries disapproved, fearing that England would be far too hedonistic. Instead, they
wished him to go to the United States.

Liholiho set sail for England in 1823, accompanied by his favorite
wife, Kamamalu.

In England, they received a mixed reception. King Liholiho was ignored by King George IV, who thought of him as a "damned savage" and
refused to grant him an audience. While Liholiho waited for his longed for
meeting with the English King, his beloved Queen Kamamalu succumbed
to measles, a disease the Hawaiians had no immunity from. King Liholiho soon followed, dying on July 14, 1824.

Their bodies were sent back to Hawaii, and the Hawaiian flag, so like
that of England, was lowered to half-mast, as the country plunged into
mourning.

# *Five*

*E*va rummaged through the medicine cabinet, opening bottles and sniffing until she came across the iodine. She winced as she dabbed it over her cuts. In the mirror she saw her ripped blouse and hair pulled loose and skin splotched orange with iodine. She quickly looked away.

From somewhere in the house she heard a shuffling noise and called out for Lehua, but there was no answer. She lit a lantern and carried it up the stairs. At the top of the stairwell the air was suddenly cooler. That wasn't right. She'd closed the window earlier in the day. She held still, listening.

To the left was a storeroom. To the right, her bedroom. She took a step towards the storeroom, then changed her mind and quickly moved towards her bedroom.

A hand reached out of the dark and took hold of her arm. A man's voice told her to be quiet, that he would explain everything but she must remain quiet.

Her legs shook with the need to run.

"Who are you?" she finally whispered.

"It doesn't matter."

She took a deep breath, and felt his hand tighten in warning. "Does Lehua know you?" she asked, her voice high and odd.

"Yes."

"How long have you been here?"

"And you're the fortuneteller, eh?" He steered her into the bedroom and closed the door behind him.

She leaned against the wall, placing her palms against the wood. "Don't touch me."

He laughed. "Do you think I am here to take advantage of you, Miss Hanson?"

She moved along the wall, edging closer to the window. She could scream, if necessary.

"This has nothing to do with you."

"Then what is it? Why are you here?" Who are you hiding from, she wondered.

He didn't answer.

"You shouldn't be here. I am in trouble with the police."

"So I've heard." He didn't sound interested. Picking up the items on her dresser, he looked closely at each object, then set it down in the exact same position.

"I will not put up with this."

"And what will you do instead?" he asked. "Lehua tells me you now have a jade necklace. You wouldn't want to lose that."

Eva drew in a breath. He was right. She didn't want to part with it. It was clearer now why Lehua had urged her to go to the police, saying that no one else could. This man needed a hiding place, and her silence had been bought with a jade necklace.

Eva started to say something, but he held his hand up. "There is also the matter of what occurred on the boat you arrived on."

Eva felt herself no longer on solid ground but back on the boat, with the movement of sea beneath her feet. "I don't feel well," she said, holding onto the windowsill.

"Then you must lie down," he said, in the same flat voice.

"You're wrong to think I won't tell anyone." Her voice was unsteady.

"It isn't in your best interests. Harboring a Hawaiian man, your customers would be scandalized. You'd have to find a new place to live. And probably another way of making a living."

He went downstairs. When she heard the back door close, she quickly dragged the dresser over to block the door, then pulled the coverlet off the bed and wrapped it around herself. She sat on the floor with her back against the dresser, thinking back to the sea voyage.

*J*t was a journey of many months, long enough for Eva to wonder what had possessed her to take a boat to the other side of the world. If it had been a train, she would have stepped off at the next station. But there were no choices on a boat. There was only time.

On the voyage, a woman in the cabin next to Eva's died suddenly. She was examined by the ship's doctor, who declared her cause of death unknown.

The dead woman had been traveling alone, with no family.

To prepare for burial, her body was bound like a mummy in a winding sheet hemmed with lead weights. The captain read a passage from the Bible, the page marked with a long black ribbon that he ran through his fingers like a small black eel. He asked if anyone had anything to say. No one did. She had died among strangers. He closed the Bible, and Eva stepped forward and tucked a small handful of seagull feathers into the winding sheet. Several of the men picked up the board the body was lying on, and with a gesture from the captain they tilted it towards the water and the body slid quickly over the side of the boat and into the sea.

The day was still. No wind pushed against the sails, the sea was perfectly clear. It was the worst sort of weather for a burial at sea. Eva stood at the railing and watched the wrapped body falling down through the water, as if watching a coffin lowered into the grave, only it did not stop there, but kept falling down through the runny soil, down into the hot liquid center of the earth.

As Eva watched, she felt part of herself pull free and follow the dead woman's path like a pilot fish, and at that moment she came up with the idea to take the woman's identity as her own.

For a great deal of money, the captain of the boat agreed to exchange Eva's papers for hers. Eva objected to his price and attempted to bargain him down, but he just winked and pointed out that losing oneself was always expensive.

Soon Eva was in possession of what she needed. It was Eva's real name that was written in the captain's logbook under deceased, her real name that followed the woman to the bottom of the ocean.

"Eva Hanson," she whispered to herself. A new name, a new beginning. Was it even possible? With a new name, she'd be much harder to find. With her past, it was just as well.

After clearing out the woman's cabin, the captain turned suddenly cheerful. The only reason Eva could think of that would change a surly, disgruntled man into a cheerful one was money. He must have pocketed the dead woman's money as well as her own, she thought.

On Sunday, as the captain led a sermon for the crew, his hand floating over the pages of the Bible like a lazy pink cloud, Eva slipped into his cabin. Her grandmother had taught her where people hid their money. Single women, between the pages of well loved books. Married women, in the kitchen, buried in a large jar of sugar or taped to the bottom of the knife drawer. Men hid money in socks, cigar humidors, or the pockets of coats left hanging at the back of a wardrobe. Yet what about the captain of a boat? Her fingers shook as she sifted through a tin of

pipe tobacco, checked his coat pockets, knocked for loose floor-
boards, unrolled his navigational charts and carefully rolled
them back up again. All she found was a daguerreotype of a sour
faced woman and a young girl next to her, sharing the same sour
look, expressions that could send a man to sea.

At dinner one night, just before their arrival in Honolulu, Eva
watched the captain as he stood up and waited to one side for
the women passengers to leave the dining room before him. He
ran his hand along the doorframe, stopping for just a moment
along the top of the frame, his fingers changing position slightly.

The next time she snuck into his cabin, Eva brought a small
wedge and a hammer, using them to pry the top of the doorframe away from the wall. The nails shrieked as they came loose
from the wood, and perspiration trickled down her chest. She
listened for footsteps along the small passageway, footsteps that
didn't come. Behind the doorframe was a small hollowed out
space. Eva reached up and felt a soft piece of fabric. A woman's
silk bag, holding enough money to take her breath away. She
weighed the bag in her hand, thought about the trouble that in-
evitably followed that much money. She pushed the silk bag
back into the empty space, and then just as quickly pulled it out
again. As greedy as the next, she scolded herself.

She sewed the dead woman's money into the wide hem of her
skirt, then weighed the silk purse down with fishing lead and
threw it into the sea.


*I*f a place is forever colored by your first view of it, Eva's view
of Oahu was of an island stretched out in the water like a bright
green lizard. As their ship sailed closer, the green separated into
cliffs and deep valleys, and the valleys separated into trees and
long streams that coursed down from the top of the mountain,
and the lizard gave a green wink and disappeared.

Eva felt her life changing, because of a green wink.

*The Floating City* · 37

As they sailed into Honolulu Harbor, men dark as insects circled their boat in dugout canoes and small dinghies. A slow rash spread across her skin. She had never seen men that dark, or that beautiful. They stared up at her from their boats, their expressions neutral.

She could barely contain her nervousness while waiting for the first class passengers to disembark. Each time the captain stepped into his cabin, a quick jolt of fear ran through her, and she silently urged everyone to hurry.

Eva couldn't believe the amount of time it was taking. Trunks and crates were unloaded first, and a man stood at the edge of the dock, holding a long list in his hands, crossing off the items as they came down the gangplank.

When she was finally allowed to disembark, she stepped onto land a richer woman, with a new name. It was August of 1894, a year and a half since Queen Lili'uokalani had been deposed, and one month since those men who'd deposed her had elected themselves to all the high offices, including president of the new Republic of Hawaii.

*T*here was a warning there, and she hadn't listened to it. But she was listening now, in the dark. A creak, a slight movement, telling her the man was now back upstairs, perhaps lying down on the futon that was kept in the storeroom.

She refused to make room for his presence, for whatever trouble he was bringing into the house. Fueled by anger, she dragged the dresser back from the wall and ran down the stairs. Lehua still wasn't home. There was only one place she'd be in the middle of the night. Eva threw on a coat and headed into town.

*A*t night, Honolulu took off one set of clothing and put on another. The tambourine-clutching evangelicals had long since ceded the stage to private clubs and noisy saloons and a tide of people washing through the streets.

There were vendors, pickpockets, drunken sailors, and the unsettling presence of American Marines. Prostitutes wore colored ribbons in their hair. Red, white, and blue. The colors of the Hawaiian flag, but those of the United States as well.

Eva ignored the attentions of the Marines and soldiers who were surprised to see a haole woman out so late at night. Someone grabbed her wrist and mockingly asked if she was in need of an escort. She pried the fingers loose, without bothering to look at the man's face.

The first opium den was locked. Eva pounded on the door until someone came from across the street and told her the place had been closed down for weeks.

"Try Chang's," he said, pointing farther down the street. "The small building with the red door."

The air was thick with smells of meat cooking, incense, mud, wilting plumeria and pikake leis on sale for half price. Clusters of people talked in low voices, with Lili'uokalani's name on everyone's lips.

Eva stepped through a drying puddle of mud and put her hand up to knock on Chang's door. It swung open before her fist touched the wood. A thin Chinese man glanced at her and then quickly slammed the door shut.

She pounded on the door. It was useless.

Nearby, a vendor cooking meat sticks over a hot fire frowned at her. She frowned back. A boy in an apron held up a tray of moist manapua buns. She couldn't remember when she'd last eaten.

After a few minutes, a large man in a long coat knocked on Chang's door. It was quickly opened, and he disappeared into the building. Eva waited. Someone else would have to go in or out.

Finally, an older woman left the building, holding the door

open long enough for Eva to push her foot across the threshold. She faced the same man.

"I'm looking for Lehua," she said.

He pushed against the air with his palms. "Not here."

"I won't leave until I see her."

He sighed, motioning her into the building.

What first hit her was the overwhelming smell of opium and incense, and something else she couldn't identify. She followed him down a low hallway with doors on either side. It was claustrophobic, like being in the hull of a very narrow boat, except there were no scratches on the walls for the passage of time.

At the end of the hall was a small bundle of fabric that turned out to be a man collapsed on the floor. The Chinese man stepped over him and pointed to a door. She opened it and entered a small dark room. As her eyes adjusted to the darkness, she saw two pallets on the floor.

She crouched down. "Lehua," she whispered.

An old man looked up at her and pointed to the other pallet. Eva steadied her breathing, and turned to the other figure.

She touched the long dark hair that was dank and heavy, spilling off the edge of the pallet. Lehua glanced at Eva, then groaned and closed her eyes.

Eva sat down next to her. "Lehua, we need to talk."

Lehua yawned.

"Why didn't you tell me about this man hiding in the house?"

Lehua shrugged and turned her face to the wall.

Eva cupped Lehua's face towards her. "I'm not part of this. You are putting me at risk by his presence." Eva shook her. "Answer me, Lehua."

"Voices carry in this building," Lehua answered.

"How could you not tell me?"

Lehua sighed. "You said yourself you didn't care about politics." She began slowly peeling the skin from her arm.

So it's political, Eva thought. "What about the police?"

"The police will never suspect you. No one would think that a haole woman would hide a Hawaiian man."

"Lehua, I'm already in trouble."

"No you're not. You're haole."

"This isn't a situation where race matters," Eva said angrily.

Lehua half propped herself up on one arm and finally looked at Eva. "You don't know anything at all. Race always matters."

Eva was furious. "Is that why you rented me a room? So you could hide people without the police knowing?"

"Think what you like." Lehua pulled up a thin blanket and closed her eyes.

Eva left her there, lying on the pallet. She wondered if Lehua would remember anything that had been said by this time tomorrow.

*In the beginning was the word, but in Hawaii the word turned out to be sugar. The road from missionary to plantation owner ran smoother than one might think.*

*Kamehameha the Great had warned his people not to sell land to foreigners, who would swoop down like birds and take the last seed from the plant, and yet by 1848 a missionary named Judd had convinced Kamehameha III to allow foreigners to purchase land by threatening the King that unless ownership of land was made available to foreigners, the United States wouldn't protect Hawaii if another country were to invade.*

*Ownership of land traditionally belonged to royalty, and to the ali'i. Those chiefs in turn made their land available for the people to use. Ownership by commoners was unheard of in Hawaii, though King Kamehameha III was finally convinced that it was good for the country.*

*Judd's next legislative bill enabled missionaries to buy land at a tremendous discount. The majority of native Hawaiians didn't have enough money to buy land, but the missionaries did. Thousands of acres were purchased by missionaries, at reduced prices unavailable to native Hawaiians. When the dust settled from the Great Mahele land division, the native Hawaiian people owned less than five percent of their country.*

# Six

Suspicious times create susceptible people, and Eva decided to take advantage of it by selling cures. She bought empty pill jars and labels and glue, and as Malia rolled the sugar pills, Eva carefully labeled the bottles. There were pills for the lovesick. For prosperity. To cure gout. She debated offering a pill that would make the Americans disappear, but thought the demand would far exceed supply.

Malia was teaching Eva the names of colors in Hawaiian. "Melemele," she instructed, as her small plump hands carefully rolled the colored sugar syrup into pills. 'Oma'oma'o was a green almost turning to yellow.

Malia named the red pills Hana Aloha. Love magic. "Take some," she teased Eva, holding out a handful. Eva laughed and swallowed a pill. "More than one," Malia said, because, with Eva's red hair and strange blue eyes, which made the children in the neighborhood shudder, she was going to need more help than most haole wahines.

The doorbell rang and Eva gave Malia a warning glance. Her first thought was that it had to do with the man upstairs. There were two men at the door, and she recognized one as the frog-tattooed policeman from the day before. The second man was a politician, one of the black-clad members of the government. Men who had made an easy transfer from God to politics, now that the latter paid more money. Although they were no longer missionaries, they still carried a whiff of it in their clothing, long black coats that buttoned securely at the collar, and thin beards that dangled like dried seaweed down the front of their chests.

Eva turned to shoo Malia out the door, but the girl had already disappeared. They were quick learners at the orphanage.

The policeman stepped out of his shoes at the door, as was the custom, but the politician left a trail of muddy shoeprints across the wooden floor.

He glanced down at her purple skirt and frowned at the color. It was the same skirt she had sewn all the stolen money into, before leaving the boat. How simple she'd thought it would be, to take on this new self, this Eva Hanson, a woman with a skirt that dragged under the weight of money.

The politician sat down without invitation. His face looked swollen, like bread dough on the second rising.

"My name is Mr. Cornelius Rhodes." He stared at Eva, waiting for his name to register.

Eva had never heard of him.

"I want to know," he said, and then with a frown turned to include the policeman, "well, we want to know, yes, what is your connection to the drowned man you discovered on the beach."

Eva hesitated. Drowning was an uncommon death, saved mostly for drunken sailors who fell off moored boats and died several feet from the dock. But she hadn't said drowned. She'd said strangled.

A floorboard creaked upstairs. "I'm not certain what I saw," Eva said quickly.

Rhodes gave her an exasperated look. "You claim to be a seer, true? Perhaps you can explain what occurred to the poor soul."

"Was it just yourself?" the policeman asked. It was the same question he'd asked yesterday. "You were alone?"

"Yes, I was alone," she replied.

He leaned closer, the tip of his tongue moving quick as a pilot fish between his lips. "Was there anything unusual about this man?"

"Yes. He was dead."

Rhodes's face flushed. "Obvious markings on the body, Miss Hanson. Anything that could clearly identify him."

"Mr. Rhodes. I did not disrobe the man," she said, and he turned slightly pinker.

"Just answer the question, Miss Hanson," the policeman scolded, but he was clearly amused at Rhodes's discomfort.

"Any papers, identification?"

He was too hungry for information, too connected to the dead man in some way.

Eva shook her head no.

"Identification?" he repeated.

A jade necklace wrapped tight as a vine around his wrist. "There was nothing." Eva waved her hand in front of her face, the way impatient people in this country did, a movement used to shoo away flies.

"Was he a Royalist?"

She hoped the man upstairs was listening. Here's the one you want, she could say, pointing straight up at the ceiling. So why not? Because it would make even more trouble, she answered herself. Besides, she had never turned anyone in to the police and didn't intend to start now.

"Answer the question, Miss Hanson. Do you think he was a Royalist?"

"Is there a way of telling a dead man's loyalties?"

"Watch yourself," the policeman warned, but he was not looking at Eva.

A room is made smaller by dislike. Between the three of them, the room was shrinking down to nothing.

Rhodes put on a pair of spectacles and picked up a bottle of red Hana Aloha pills. He squinted at the label, then shook his head. "These are false claims."

Eva shrugged. Did it matter? A man with an amputated leg still felt pain in his missing foot.

"Absolute heresy," he said.

"Only if you believe it," she answered.

The policeman smiled and then just as quickly frowned.

"It is against the law, Miss Hanson. Magic claims and potions. You people seem intent on sending us back to the Dark Ages."

And where does that put you, Eva wondered. You could do far worse than to swallow a few Hana Aloha pills.

His expression suddenly tightened. "You are ambitious."

Was this meant as an accusation? Of course she was ambitious. "We must all make our living," she answered. Her grandmother Mormor always said that a woman couldn't afford independence, and she was finally beginning to understand what that meant.

He drummed the table with manicured hands, a half moon visible under each nail. Vain hands, she thought.

No one spoke. The rain went from a drizzle to a downpour, and Eva was relieved. It would cover any sounds the man upstairs might make.

Rhodes looked out the window and Eva followed his glance. Next door, Tomas was scurrying to bring in his laundry, his wet undergarments sagging like white flags of surrender.

"How well did you know the deceased?" Rhodes suddenly asked.

"I did not know him," she said slowly, the way one spoke to a child, so that each word would be clearly received. "I have never seen him before in my life."

He leaned his head sideways and the flesh on his face followed. "Come, now. Every person in this town believes he knows the deceased. When someone in Honolulu dies, at least a hundred people show up to identify him." He turned to the policeman. "Isn't that true?"

The policeman looked uncomfortable.

Eva turned to him. "So you have found the body."

"Yes," he said, without glancing at Rhodes.

He is lying, she thought. But why?

The walls were still moving in, squeezing the three of them together into some unfortunate pattern she couldn't make sense of. Nothing good would come of it.

Cornelius Rhodes's fingers drummed a little louder. Upstairs, there was a shuffling noise that Eva covered by coughing long enough that the policeman offered her a handkerchief.

"A little peculiar that you'd be the one to stumble across him, isn't it?"

"The dead have no control over who finds them."

"You're quite certain you didn't know him? Perhaps even know him quite well?"

"That's ridiculous."

The policeman started in. "Did the deceased make a promise to you? A marriage proposal?"

Eva sighed. They were poor collaborators. Neither of them for a moment believed that anyone would marry a woman as disreputable as a red haired fortuneteller.

"And when he jilted you, something happened to him?"

"Oh, yes," she said, "it was the love affair of the century. And then of course he broke my heart."

Rhodes glanced at the policeman. There was an unspoken communication between them, and Eva instantly regretted her rashness. She needed to think before she spoke to this man, she needed to pay closer attention.

"Well, as you stated, you were alone with the body."

"I was alone."

Despite their questions, they were well aware that she didn't know the dead man. So what was this about? They were worried, Eva suddenly realized, that she might have recognized him. So who was he? A Royalist? A high-level politician with a mistress who tied a jade necklace around his wrist and a rope around his neck and then pushed him into the water?

"You have a reason to be alone on a deserted beach?"

"Yes. I fish."

They looked at her skeptically. The truth so rarely worked. Something fell over upstairs. Rhodes glanced up at the ceiling, and Eva held her breath until he looked back down at her. "Do you realize we have witnesses who've said that you knew the deceased?"

"And who would those witnesses be? Your drunken American Marines?"

The tendons on his neck were suddenly visible. "Reliable witnesses," he said, trying to keep his voice under control. He pushed himself away from the table and stood up. "Someone has to be responsible."

The policeman shook his head in warning. "Pull yourself together," he said in a low voice.

Rhodes took out a handkerchief that was already wet and mopped his face with it.

"I found him," Eva said softly. "It doesn't therefore mean that I knew him. You must realize I came of my own free will to the police station." Nearly. Last night, she had shown the piece of jade to a jeweler who dealt in stolen goods. He told her that he would have a buyer within a month, unless the piece was well known. In that case, they would need to send it to the United States to sell. He'd offered to keep it for her, but she'd hesitated, not wanting to let it out of her sight.

"Would I go to the police if I were somehow connected to this man?"

"No, Miss Hanson," the policeman said quickly. "It was good of you to come forward."

"Well, thank you," Eva answered. "It's just what any responsible person would do." English was the perfect language for deceit. It was like water, it took on the shape of whatever it was poured into.

Just as she believed she was winning, they changed direction.

"You had reasons to leave Norway in a hurry?" Rhodes asked in a voice that made her feel like she was six years old again, backing out of a shop with a stolen egg in her pocket and every merchant in town knowing to keep an eye out for the red haired girl with hands like eels.

"No reason at all," she said, but of course there was. It was that old game of warmer and colder. Did you know the dead man was a cold question. Leaving Norway in a hurry was a warm question. And the answer was right there in the hand-painted tarot cards, if anyone bothered to look.

They stepped out of the room, to talk between themselves.

Eva stood up and tiptoed to the door, straining to overhear. Her reflection wavered in the small mirror hanging on the opposite wall, her mouth dyed bright red from the Hana Aloha pills. The mouth of a clown, she thought, rubbing her lips with the back of her hand.

Yet what about Eva Hanson? She remembered looking through a small leather suitcase the woman had left behind, trying to find some sense of who she was, or where she came from, but all she'd found were ticket stubs showing that the woman had crisscrossed Europe, and a love letter with so many passages inked out that Eva wondered why the woman had bothered to keep it. At the time it seemed like aimless wandering, the sort someone with money and a broken heart might have done.

Now she worried that it wasn't a love letter at all, but a code of some kind and a woman running away from trouble. And people never start running until they see the size of the dog chasing them.

She wondered at her naïveté in taking the identity of a complete stranger. Your inventions should carry you to the moon and back, but they never do. People are only capable of taking a few steps from the self they have so eagerly discarded. What bad luck, she thought, to purchase the identity of a woman with problems greater than her own.

"Miss Hanson, I am speaking to you."

Eva glanced up, startled.

"We have the name of the ship you arrived on. We believe the captain will have information about you."

She took this in without answering. Her hands felt like they were leaking water. She glanced down at her lucky skirt, which no longer dragged with money, not even enough for a bribe.

"Is something bothering you, Miss Hanson?"

"Nothing at all."

"You're certain you have nothing to say to us?"

Eva remembered once watching a group of children gathered around a drunken man, and one boy had knelt down with a box of matches and set the man's shoes on fire. Perhaps Rhodes had been that sort of child.

"We'll have to ask you to stay in Honolulu, at least until this matter is resolved," the policeman said.

"Of course," she agreed, vowing to leave on the next boat if she could come up with the fare.

Rhodes threw a coin down on the table. "For my fortune," he said.

"Keep your money," she answered, but he was already through the door.

She picked up the coin, rolled it across the table, and watched it bounce over the edge and fall to the floor. Tails.

*O*ld whalers with tattoos falling into the folds of their flesh filled every corner of Honolulu. Their tattoos were of conquests, real and imagined: sea creatures and women and faded flags of countries they hadn't seen in years. In the late 1840s, there were over six hundred whaling ships coming regularly to Hawaii, but in 1859, a new kind of oil lamp was invented in Pennsylvania, using oil from a well rather than whale oil. The discovery soon ended the whaling industry, and since then the whalers found themselves surrounded by the treacherous reefs of leisure time, with lives that would end on land.

# Seven

$\mathcal{E}$va fingered the coin from the politician, then set it on the windowsill. There was a movement behind her, and she turned, expecting Malia.

Instead, it was the man who'd spent the night in the storeroom. In daylight, he threw off half his years and Eva found herself staring at someone younger than she was. Tousled hair and an old palaka shirt with coconut buttons.

He came into the kitchen and watched Eva cutting a loaf of sweet bread. Without thinking, she handed him a piece.

He nodded his thanks and ate the bread quickly.

She offered him a second piece, and he declined, though it was obvious he was still hungry.

She introduced herself. He hesitated a moment, then told her that his name was Jonathan.

This wasn't a coin Eva needed to bite down on to know it was false. "Jonathan. Why have you picked a haole name?"

"It is easier to pronounce," he answered, sounding irritated. "People who come here aren't usually interested in learning our language."

"Well, I don't see that anyone is learning the language of my country, either."

"We are not in your country, Miss Hanson."

Eva flushed.

"Who were those men?" he asked.

"Friends of yours, for all I know."

"No, you're mistaken if you think that."

At least he's not with the police, Eva thought. "You're lucky I didn't tell them about you."

"And what would you have said?" He sounded amused.

She ignored his question. "What is it you want?"

"I want you to go on as usual," he said. "Do everything as you would normally do."

She almost laughed. What would he consider normal? The police with their eye on her, and a politician named Rhodes, and now a man with a false name, hiding in Lehua's storeroom?

"What makes you think I can be trusted?" she asked.

"You misunderstand, Miss Hanson," he answered formally. "It isn't a question of trust. Neither of us wants trouble with the people who are temporarily in charge of this country. For different reasons, obviously," he added.

He was referring to the jade. "Well." She was unable to keep the anger out of her voice. "As long as we understand each other."

"Yes, I think we do. A compromise. And I will only be here for a very short time."

*E*va fed the new laces through her boot eyelets, slipped them on, pulled tight into a double knot. A compromise? No. She'd had enough. This island was no longer a safe haven for her. Now it was a series of wrong turns and mistakes, and a smart person would be on the next boat out. It was time to find Edward and borrow enough money to leave. And take the jade with her, save on the commission she'd otherwise have to pay the jeweler.

Yet, on the street, she remembered how she'd felt when she first arrived in Honolulu.

Those early days had been marked by what she learned to take off. Outer crinoline, immediately. Jacket, stays, corset, all of it quickly left behind like the husk of a cicada. She'd been on board the ship for such a long time that the island swayed under her feet. She had a restlessness that made her look in four directions at once, made her long for sweet as soon as sour was on her tongue.

She spent her time walking through a town she could hardly believe. A confusion of children the rich colors of soil and polished wood raced barefoot through the crowds, delivering food and messages. Pale Americans looked like they had somehow wandered into the wrong landscape. A man wearing sandwich boards advertised the joys of sarsaparilla in Hawaiian and English, and women sat on woven mats surrounded by baskets of fragrant plumeria flowers, stringing endless leis.

Honolulu was crisscrossed with mud streets and wooden sidewalks, and the smell of freshly cut wood was everywhere. Sawdust powdered the damp bodies of carpenters who'd gone from shipbuilding to the making of endless coffins for those who were quickly dying from leprosy, smallpox, measles, venereal disease.

Everyone in Honolulu gambled, whether for souls or lottery numbers or how many days before the mango trees bloomed, or the arrival of the iceboats.

It was a town where the exact date of the arrival of the mosquito could be pinpointed to a ship that years ago had carried infected water and thrown it overboard into a small river ripe for infestation, but no one could pinpoint the moment that the political world began unraveling and the leadership of the country was snatched up by foreign businessmen and missionaries. It was enough to make a person dizzy, to make anyone lose his balance.

Shrieking evangelicals beat tin drums and lit fires in small black kettles that were meant to represent hell. Young children crouched down and threw geckos and centipedes into the flames, and watched closely as the creatures disappeared in a wiggling flash of smoke, while above them the evangelists, tendons jumproping across their necks, remained blind to the actual hell expanding at their feet.

Eva was amazed by the beauty of the women, and how so many of them were streetwalkers. She'd never before seen salvation and prostitution in such close proximity.

What did she feel? Free. She was a stranger walking down a strange street in a town no one could find her in. Everything that had hurt her was left behind, on the other side of the world.

She carried a newspaper with an advertisement for a room for rent. By mistake, she arrived at a home for retired sailors, a dilapidated cottage with a tin roof and ferns growing out of the rain gutter.

Tomas sat on the lanai with a rooster on his lap. He told her the rooster's name before he said his own. "Lucky," he said, holding up the bird that was strangely calm in his hands. "Since no one has eaten him yet," he added with a toothless smile.

Eva held out her newspaper and showed him where she had circled the advertisement.

He cleared his throat. "I never knew reading," he apologized. "Tell me what it says."

A single woman with rooms to rent to women.

"Ah, that's Lehua. Next door. Let's see. Women only, and no Americans."

"I'm not American," Eva said. "I'm Norwegian."

He stood up and the bird fluttered to the ground. "I never took you for an American," he assured her.

She found the path through the hedge and met Lehua, a Hawaiian woman whose smile lifted the edges of her mouth like Aladdin's lamp.

There was an orphanage for Hawaiian girls across the street, and old whalers next door with a pet rooster. There was the Widow, locally famous for outliving all her husbands and winning the orchid show every year for the last twenty-two years, and a shamisen player who made enough racket to drive away the living as well as the dead. There was Lehua, who was half out of her mind with grief and opium, and for the first time in her life, Eva fit right in.

*O*r so it seemed at the time. Now everything had changed, as if she'd fallen asleep in one country and woken up in another.

Outside the brothels, the bamboo cages were haphazardly stacked against the walls. The cages were crowded with birds and small animals, some noisy with fear, others struck dumb with lassitude or ill health. A birdcage filled with mynahs was placed just above the cage of a mongoose, ensuring a complete frenzy. On the sidewalk, a chimpanzee's small hands shot through the bars of the cage to grab hold of Eva's skirt as she passed by. The brothel owner smiled at her shocked reaction, and with the tip of his boot he prodded the cage a little farther into the street.

It reminded her of Tomas's story of the whale who lifted its back out of the sea and was mistaken for an island. He hadn't told the girls from the orphanage the rest of the story. The sailor's anchors caught like hooks under the flesh of the whale, and they lit fires to cook dinner. When the whale felt the heat of the fire, it dove down and dragged the sailors and their anchored ships after it.

Along this street the fires had all been lit.

She passed a streetcorner missionary, a thin man wearing a shiny coat and a pair of boots for a man twice his size. "It's in the air," he proclaimed, "Honolulu is rampant with wickedness."

He shook his finger at her purple skirt, her loose hair, glaring down with a face as mottled as the inside of a biscuit, and she sensed that the evil he'd previously attached to the air of Honolulu had now found a new target.

As she came closer to Edward's office, the street widened. Alongside the road, small trees were planted in measured intervals and picket fences skirted the tidy lawns of the missionaries.

Their grand houses were the sort that as a child Eva had imagined herself living in one day, before she knew how wildly unsuitable her family was, with their gypsy colored clothes, their reputation on them like a smell they could not wash away.

But what of the luxury of these houses, the true cost of the chandeliers that trembled around the Horn, the wood that was carried out of the forests of the Philippines on an old man's back, the tablecloths that sent an Irish lacemaker into blindness? Eva rejected that world. Edward was embracing it.

When she'd first moved to Honolulu, she'd noticed Edward in a bar one night. She watched him cheating at cards and getting away with it. He looked up, saw Eva watching him closely, winked, and sent a drink her way.

At that time, he was a bartender, and also a procurer. He arranged for his customers to have whatever they could afford to pay for. Opium, prostitutes, gambling. Since then, he'd moved into politics, claiming that it was the same game, dressed up in finer clothing.

His office was at the end of a row of modest wooden buildings. An older woman sat against the wall on a small lauhala mat spread over the dirt. Eva recognized her as the woman who moved her produce up and down the street, seeking the coolness of shade. Today she had four lilikois for sale. Why only four? Eva crouched down and picked out the yellowest fruit and paid the woman.

Edward's outer room was empty except for a row of benches and broken umbrellas leaning against the wall. She knocked on the door to his office and without asking who it was, he told her to wait.

She sat down on a bench against the wall, willing herself to appear at ease. Trouble was as easy to smell as poverty, and Edward wanted nothing to do with either.

Eventually, the door to his office opened and a woman with a florid face and disheveled hair walked past Eva, pretending not to see her.

Edward was at his desk, busy copying figures into a ledger. Seeing that it was Eva, he set down his pen and regarded her fondly.

"Edward," she said. "You will never change."

"I hope not," he answered happily.

"Who is she?"

He held his finger to his lips and they both laughed.

"I miss you, Eva," he said suddenly.

Eva smiled. "Yes, I can see that. You appear miserable."

She set the lilikoi down on his desk. "Here, this is for you."

He picked it up. "How thoughtful of you. What is it?"

"It's a lilikoi, Edward. A fruit with lots of seeds. Makes a delicious juice."

"Ah, I see. You realize that you are supporting the woman who begs outside my office."

"She's not begging, Edward. She's selling fruit."

"Sure she is. So, how are things with you? How is Lehua? Still smoking opium?"

"Not at all," she lied.

"No?"

"Hasn't touched it in weeks. And yourself, Edward. How is the political life?"

"Good, but at the same time very peculiar. The politicians here? They'd think this country was paradise if they could just figure out how to get rid of the Hawaiians."

"That's disgusting."

"It is, isn't it? I've never seen anything like it." He shrugged. "Do you have any idea, Eva, how many young daughters these missionary politicians have? And all of them looking for husbands. White husbands, mind you. Only haoles. No Hawaiians need apply."

"And you are ingratiating yourself."

"I certainly hope to. You may find them disgusting, but Eva, think of how powerful they are. Think of the money."

Eva nodded. She had.

"They control more of this country than you think." He shook his head. "They even call themselves Hawaiians now. It's insidious." He laughed and pulled a cigar from his pocket.

She preferred Edward back when he was a gambler, a cardsharp who would lift money from the pocket of a sleeping drunk and buy a round of drinks for the house. To her, it was still more honest than politics.

"But I am not here just to visit, Edward."

He pretended to be surprised. "No? Eva, I hate to bring up old business, but I should remind you that you still haven't paid me back from the last time."

"Well, yes. But you know my business is seasonal."

Edward smiled, enjoying her discomfort. "Is it, now?"

"You have my word that I'll pay you back."

"Yes, that's my fear. I have your word. Not much to go on."

"How is business, Edward?"

"Unfortunately, these are slow times for me as well."

Eva sighed. "You always do something peculiar with your neck when you're lying—did you know that, Edward? I can't quite say what it is. Your Adam's apple moves about too much."

"Do I?" He laughed, placing his hand over his throat. "I'll have to watch that."

"Lehua has promised to include me in the Queen's weekly card games. It will help tremendously. I'm sure to find many new clients there."

"What the Queen needs isn't a fortuneteller or a card game.

She needs an army. This government has tied her hands behind her back, and they're still scared of her."

"They should be," Eva answered.

"They are spreading the worst sort of rumors about Lili'uokalani. They're even saying that . . ."

Eva held up her hand. "I don't want to hear rumors," she interrupted. "They say whatever they think furthers their cause. It only makes them appear stupider than before."

"Don't underestimate them, Eva." He set his cigar in the ashtray. "You realize that things are heating up. Be careful which side you're standing on."

"I don't stand on either side, Edward, and neither do you."

"True enough. We might be the only two people in Honolulu who aren't pretending that this country belongs to us. But enough of all that. What's on your mind?"

"Edward, we've helped each other out quite a few times in the past," Eva began.

"Not always successfully," he answered, but he was smiling.

"No," she agreed, "not always."

"You got caught, didn't you? What has happened, Eva?"

"Nothing, really. I mean, I've done nothing. There is a situation, though."

"A situation."

"There are lists of the dead, aren't there?"

"Yes, the police would have that information."

Eva waved that idea aside. "I don't want to involve the police."

"Always a good policy."

"The other day I went fishing, down along the coast. And I found a body."

"A body?"

"A man. Washed in from the sea." Eva paused. If she told Edward that the man had been strangled, he wouldn't help her at all. Not for murder. "He was a young man," she continued, "or maybe middle-aged. Mostly Hawaiian, but perhaps a little Chinese. He had long black hair. He was handsome," she added, surprising herself.

"A handsome dead man, really?" He leaned forward, interested. "If he was Chinese, what rights he has are negligible. In this town, if you find a dead man you'd better pick his race carefully."

"Edward, you sound like one of them."

"I do, don't I? It starts to rub off on you. But why should a dead Chinese man concern you?"

"I don't know. He just does." She couldn't tell Edward that there might be a reward, because he'd try to claim it for himself.

"Was there anything on the body? Anything in his pockets?"

"I didn't look."

He raised his eyebrows in disbelief, knowing she'd never let an opportunity like that pass by.

"So, another drowned man," he shrugged. "Someone who drank too much or smoked too much opium and fell into the sea."

"Yes, it appeared that way at first. But when I took the police to where I'd left the body, it was no longer there."

"So who cares about a missing body?"

"Generally, no one does, at least in this town."

"So why not drop it? Or is there something else?"

"Well, yes. The policeman came to my house the next day. A follow-up visit, I suppose. Except that there was another person with him."

"Eva. Just tell me what happened."

"The other man was a politician." She told him about the policeman and the politician coming to her home. All of it except the jade necklace.

"Why would a politician be involved?"

She shrugged. "I don't know."

Edward stood up and moved to the window. "Unless," he finally said, "the dead man was a Royalist. In which case it could be murder. No wonder they're paying attention to you." He sounded worried, and she knew he wouldn't help her if it would hurt his career.

"I don't know who the politician was, he didn't give his name," she lied.

"What did he look like?"

"A haole man with skin like a jellyfish." That much was true, at least.

"Sounds charming. Do you remember what party he was with?"

Eva shook her head. There were more political parties than she could keep track of.

"This sounds like trouble," he warned.

Eva was suddenly exasperated. "I did not kill the man, Edward, I just found him."

He leaned forward, placing his hands on the desk. "Does it matter? You are connected."

"No, I am not. They want me to be connected, which is what I don't understand." She paused. This was the moment for Edward to offer to help. But why should he? "Edward, couldn't you ask a few discreet questions, try to find out something?"

He gestured towards his papers. "As you can see, I'm quite busy. Tell you what, when I find the time, I'll look into it."

She sighed. The cautious Edward had taken over. It was probably better not to ask about boat fares. That would have to wait for a more opportune moment.

"This town is heating up," he said, motioning her towards the door.

"You repeat yourself, Edward. And I think you worry too much."

"And you clearly don't worry enough."


*O*n the street Eva saw a prostitute she knew well, a woman who had been one of her steadiest customers until the birth of her son. You know what your future is now, Eva had told her at their last meeting. The woman assured Eva that she would not be long in the business, which was what all the prostitutes said, but often they were supporting entire families and couldn't afford to quit.

Today she proudly held her palms apart to show how much her baby had grown. As they hugged goodbye, Eva felt the bones in the woman's back, knowing that the venereal disease that had already taken so many Hawaiian women was now claiming her as well.

An uneasy feeling came over Eva. She turned and looked back at Edward's office.

He was standing in the doorway watching her, and when their eyes met he nodded slightly before ducking back into his office. She realized that he wasn't worried for himself, he was worried for her.

*E*veryone points to someone else as the cause of the country's woes. Sailors blame the missionaries, the missionaries blame the opium dealers, sugar cane planters blame the rulings of the legislature, and the legislators blame the end of the American Civil War, which poured Southern sugar back into the market. The prostitutes blame the foreigners for bringing the kiss of death, and everyone else blames the Chinese.

# Eight

$\mathcal{I}$olani Palace sat in the middle of Honolulu with its face turned towards the sea. The building was half European, half tropical. There were pillars and a grand entry, but at the same time the palace could only exist in Hawaii, with an outside veranda running the length of the building, and tall shuttered windows that opened to the trade winds and the light.

It was built during the reign of Lili'uokalani's brother, King Kalakaua, and the legislature let the King know that they disapproved of the expense. Kalakaua ignored them.

Eva walked up to the gates of the palace. Winding her fingers between the metal bars, she remembered her first glimpse of Queen Lili'uokalani, in August of the previous year. Eva had only been in the islands for a few weeks, when Lehua invited her to meet the Queen. Lili'uokalani had been deposed since January 1893, and although it was well known that the new government spied on her, she was still allowed a certain amount of freedom.

It was on a day so bright the sun turned the ocean into a mirror. The Queen was on the beach in Waikiki, standing in the middle of a cluster of large black rocks. As Lehua and Eva walked closer, the rocks separated themselves into women in muumuus sitting on the sand, and missionary wives sitting on portable chairs. Several of the women were emptying sand out of their shoes, and it was as if these women were in charge of the passage of time, each shoe clocking another hour as the sand fell out of it.

Eva came before Lili'uokalani, and dropped into a nervous curtsy. She had practiced it again and again in front of Lehua, but now her long purple skirt was damp in the sea air and the fabric twisted around her legs like a stubborn vine, and the heat rushed to her face as she stumbled and took a step backwards.

Lili'uokalani nodded, smiling softly at Eva's difficulty, and she held her arms open for Lehua, whom she'd first met as a child in the orphanage. The Queen was as regal as Eva had expected, yet she had an open face, and hands that Eva instantly trusted, hands that moved like dancers at the ends of her arms.

"You come from far away, Miss Hanson," the Queen said.

"Norway, Your Highness." Towns that had passed in a blur of stolen pocket watches and purses.

"I admire you. It isn't easy for women to travel," the Queen said, looking suddenly more interested.

"Why would anyone bother to travel?" one of the Queen's women asked in a bored voice.

"I would like to travel," the Queen said. "But I am prevented from either ruling or leaving my country."

There was an awkward silence. Eva and Lehua sat down at the edge of the group. Eva's shoes filled with sand and she smiled at all the women who did not return her smile. The ocean hissed at her back, but no louder than the thoughts of those around her. All publicity was bad for fortunetellers, they simply expected it. Even a stray dog knew that theirs was the leg to bite.

The Hawaiian women were curious about her, with her strange accent and her dark red hair, but the missionary wives were dismissive. Several of them made a point of moving away from Eva. The sand was wet, and the women dragged their chairs like someone plowing backwards, leaving wide trails in the sand like the tracks of large sea turtles.

She tallied what she would make telling the fortunes of these women, and she smiled at them all, especially those who had dragged their chairs the farthest away. In Norway it was said that the largest bear makes the biggest splash.

Several of the Hawaiian women cradled ukuleles, and when they began to sing, it was a song written by Lili'uokalani. The Hawaiian language had a round, smooth sound, whereas Norwegian was all right turns, narrow alleys, a sharp boot kicking a shin. In Norwegian there was a sound that stuck a blade in your back and turned it. There was no sound for this in Hawaiian.

Every so often Eva felt Lili'uokalani's eyes on her, and when she dared to look, the Queen gave her the same soft smile.

If the Queen approved of her, Eva would have all the clients she needed.

A woman named Betty suddenly leaned forward and addressed Eva. "You're good at guessing the future, are you?"

"I never guess," Eva lied. "I simply know it or I don't."

"Then what does Margaret's future hold?" Betty pointed her fan at a well dressed young woman who flushed at the sudden attention.

Eva's first thought was marriage, but that was too obvious, too easy. She knew the girl's future wouldn't be her own decision. How many futures were available for a girl of her class? The more money, the fewer choices.

"Missionary school," she guessed, and from the shocked silence, she knew she was correct.

Only one person laughed, and it was the Queen. "Maika'i loa. Very good," she said. Eva felt the air change when Lili'uokalani laughed, everything around them moving a little closer.

"And now you must tell my fortune," she said.

The Queen's future looked as grim as her recent past. Eva felt her throat tighten. She had no wish to speak of such a miserable future.

Lehua suddenly spoke up, rescuing her. "Eva needs time to think about such an important future," she said, addressing Lili'uokalani. "Perhaps she could turn her sights onto another person?"

Lili'uokalani nodded, and the woman seated next to her raised her fan.

"Your future is secure," Eva said.

The woman looked pleased. "And how do you come to that decision?" she asked.

"Because you are sitting next to the Queen," Eva answered, and Lili'uokalani laughed again.

They took their leave soon after. Eva felt eyes on her as she walked across the sand. She turned and glanced back once, saw the trail of her boots marking the sand like the hulls of boats.

"Why didn't you want to tell the Queen's future?" Lehua asked.

"Ah, Lehua. I couldn't see much, to tell the truth," Eva admitted. "But I can't help thinking the political situation will only become worse for the Queen."

"I think so as well," Lehua said.

They walked up onto the road that ran parallel to the sea, and as soon as they were out of sight of the women they jumped up and down to shake the sand from their clothes.

"The Queen likes you, you know. She likes people who take chances. And don't think her interest in you wasn't noticed by the missionary wives," Lehua warned, but Eva, now busy adding up imaginary sums of money, wasn't listening.

*A*lmost two years had passed since the Queen had lost her throne in January 1893. Eva wound her fingers through the empty bars of the palace gates. The gates had once held the

Hawaiian coat of arms. The plaques had read: Ua Mau Ke Ea O Ka Aina I Ka Pono. The Life of the Land Is Perpetuated in Righteousness.

Lehua had told her that the word iolani meant royal hawk. 'Io was the hawk that was disappearing from the islands. Lani was royal or heavenly. Iolani. Palace of the Royal Hawk. Hawaiian was turning into a language haunted by loss.

There was suddenly the sound of a horn, followed by a flute. And then enough instruments to know that it was a band, warming up. Eva followed the music, and when she turned the corner she was surprised to see the Royal Hawaiian Band gathered on the side lawn of the palace.

A crowd quickly gathered, drawn simply for the oddity of hearing the royal band playing on property that was now considered headquarters for the new government.

The bandleader, a large German man with a fondness for epaulets and braided loops, stood behind a podium at the front of the Coronation Pavilion.

They played a tune, and the bandleader, one of Lili'uokalani's closest friends, told those gathered that he was playing the Queen's songs as a protest. A show of solidarity by those who wanted the monarchy and the Queen reinstated.

"Who are these men," he asked, "who have named themselves the leaders of this country?"

"Haoles from the United States," a man in the crowd answered.

Eva glanced around nervously. This wasn't staying out of trouble, as she'd been warned.

The dry wind picked up, and overhead the rows of palms rustled. As the musicians began the next song, the doors to the palace swung open and the soldiers of the Republic of Hawaii marched down the steps. A nervous ripple passed through the crowd.

The band was told that they could not play without a permit.

The musicians shifted their weight, eyed each other uneasily, but the bandleader shook his head and said he only took orders from the Queen.

The soldier in charge replied that the palace was the property of the government and that everyone on the palace grounds was now trespassing.

A young man from the United States, the bandleader pointed out, telling a crowd of Hawaiian people that they were trespassing.

Eva kept her eye on the soldier, thinking he should be ashamed, but at the same time knowing that to put a man in uniform was to blind him in one eye.

The bandleader nodded to his musicians, then raised his baton. They played a song written by Lili'uokalani. The late afternoon sun wavered across the glass of the palace windows, and the soldiers stood in a crooked line, uncertain what to do next.

As the song ended, a Hawaiian man in ragged clothing climbed onto a wall and walked the length of it, balancing with his arms held out to the sides. For a moment Eva saw the black crows of her childhood, perched along fence lines that went on longer than a person's life.

The man cheered for Lili'uokalani and the crowd answered him. A woman carrying a Hawaiian flag was hoisted onto the shoulders of others, and another cheer went up. Before she knew what she was doing, Eva found herself cheering along with them.

A soldier waved his gun in the face of the bandleader, yelling that he'd be taken to jail if he didn't stop playing. Immediately. The bandleader pushed him to the side, and as the musicians began another song, a scuffle broke out. The crowd circled and pressed forward as if at a cockfight, and the bandleader yelled something in German as two soldiers dragged him off through the crowd.

On the opposite side of the Coronation Pavilion, Eva caught a glimpse of Jonathan. When she looked again, he was gone.

Suddenly everyone was fighting, pushing against the soldiers. Three shots were fired into the air, and the crowd panicked. People picked up small children, anyone's children, and ran with them slung over their shoulders. The woman next to Eva looked down at her bloodcovered palms and screamed.

She stumbled, taking Eva down with her. A foot pressed against her ankle and she felt it give way under the weight and then everything turned black.

Hands reached under her arms and lifted her off the ground. As soon as she stood, a sharp pain ran up her leg. A tall man told her they had to run, but she couldn't. He put his arm around her waist to support her.

The soldiers were dragging people towards the jail and so they ran in the opposite direction, across the lawn of the palace. When they reached the street, she crouched down to undo the laces of her boot, on the verge of fainting from the pain.

Trampled flowers littered the street. A wooden lei stand hung in splinters. Orchids, plumerias, a bright red petal that had been soaked in dye. In the dusk, the street had turned liquid, and the flowers looked like those that washed in from the boats leaving Honolulu Harbor.

"Here." The man leaned down with a bag of fruit from one of the abandoned carts. "Please," he said, and she realized he was Scottish. As he handed her the bag, she noticed his rough hands and looked up at his face.

He was tall, fair-haired, with the soft coloring of a young boy, the coloring people usually grew out of. Yet his profile was sharp as a bird of prey. She liked it that parts of his face were at war, and that liking caught her so suddenly that she was confused by it and quickly looked back down at the bag of fruit.

They were both covered in dirt, and the hem of her skirt dragged on the ground like a ribbon. She was hungry and ate the berries quickly, her hands staining with juice.

A young soldier approached, carrying his gun like a school

trophy. He stopped in front of them, and the man sitting next to her stiffened.

The soldier told them that the curfew began in five minutes. "You'll want to get your wife home, sir," he added.

Eva laughed.

"What curfew?" the man asked, trying to keep the anger out of his voice.

The soldier frowned at him, his grip tightening around his gun. "Martial law has just been declared. Anyone on the street goes to jail."

"How long will the curfew last?" Eva asked, trying to take the soldier's attention away from the Scot.

"As long as necessary," the soldier replied. "There are rumors that the Royalists are planning something. Stay off the streets."

The Scot turned to her, his large hand waving a circle in the hot air. "There are always rumors about the Royalists," he said, for the soldier's benefit.

The soldier shifted uncomfortably. "Well, I'll be leaving you, then."

Neither of them answered.

The Scot stood up, offering her a hand.

"Who are you?" she asked, once the soldier was out of earshot.

He shook her hand and gave a funny little bow. "Name is McClelland, ma'am. Very pleased to meet you."

Mc-Clel-land, she said to herself, breaking his name into pieces, then putting it together again.

When she stood up, her leg buckled from the pain, and she took his arm for support.

He had a green smell, like crushed leaves. There were stupider reasons for letting someone help you down the street. She'd once held her own hand out to a frightened child with ice cracking around her skates. Trust me, her hand said. Don't trust your own feet.

"We should get off the main road."

"You believe what he said about the curfew?" Around them, the shadows were moving as fast as spilled ink.

"It appears that everyone else does. The town is nearly empty."

A woman ran towards them, her muumuu plastered against her in the heat. "My keiki," she said.

McClelland stopped in the road. "What about your child?"

"She is lost. We don't live in Honolulu, she won't find her way home."

"We'll help you find her," McClelland said.

Not me, Eva thought, I've had enough trouble for one day.

"We'll go in two different directions, and meet up at the fish market. Do you know where that is?"

The woman nodded. She gave the child's name and ran off, calling her.

Eva and McClelland went in the opposite direction of the woman, McClelland looking for the child, Eva looking for a long stick to make a crutch.

Along the road, brightly lit paper lanterns blew in the hot wind, round globes of color twirling like a line of planets spinning out of control. The lanterns belonged to brothels, each brothel with a different color of lantern, so that even in the stumbling dark the sailors and the sons of missionaries knew where to go.

Tonight, even the brothel that catered to the Americans was silent. On most nights it was full of drunken haole men who danced with Hawaiian women more beautiful than anyone they had ever seen, and they tipped the women with a little money, a little contagious disease. The Hawaiian women danced with the next sailors and the next missionary sons until it was clear to those men that they were dancing with ghosts, and the women were replaced with others.

Dusk and smoke covered the empty streets, and as McClelland shouted the daughter's name it echoed like a birdcall.

A small figure darted across the road and ran into a cluster of hau trees.

McClelland softly called the girl's name, and there was a faint whimpering.

"She's scared to come out," he said. He crouched down on his hands and knees.

On a nearby street was the sound of running. More soldiers, Eva thought.

A small face appeared between the leaves of the hau tree.

"Your mother told us to look for you," McClelland said softly. The girl didn't move.

Eva crouched down beside him. "Ho 'olu." Please.

The little girl climbed out and stared at them. She looked about four years old. McClelland offered his hand, and the child stared up at his face for a moment before placing her small hand carefully into his.

How do you decide to trust one person and not another, Eva wondered. It wasn't instinct at all, it was a kind of blindness.

A patrol of soldiers came out of a small shop. Without thinking, Eva crawled into the hau trees, and McClelland and the girl followed.

The soldiers were guarding an older Hawaiian man. They began arguing between themselves, pushing against each other, circling like two young bulls. The old man used the moment to break loose and run down the street.

"Good for you," McClelland whispered, and Eva glanced at him.

The soldiers halfheartedly chased after the man, but soon gave up. They lit cigarettes, their argument already forgotten. The shorter one said something in a low voice, and Eva heard bits of a joke.

He tossed his gun down several feet from where she was hiding. The joke had to do with a woman with large breasts, and his white hands palmed the air, and the other soldier laughed and bent down so close to the bushes that Eva held her breath, certain he was looking straight at her, but he just picked up the gun, and a moment later they wandered off.

"What was all that?" McClelland asked.

"A joke," Eva said, taking a deep breath. "He was telling a joke."

McClelland shrugged. "Amateurs."

Eva quickly glanced at him. If they were amateurs, she wondered, what did that make him?

When they reached the market, the mother was waiting outside the locked door. She took the child into her arms, and nodded at McClelland. "Mahalo," she said.

Around them, doors and windows were slamming shut, bolts were drawn. In the midst of all the agitation, Eva felt strangely exhilarated. There was a wind blowing and she felt herself expanding, like a sail filling with wind and moving in all directions at once.

*D*ue to serious mismanagement of finances, in 1887 King Kalakaua was forced to sign a new constitution by the predominantly American born legislature. The new constitution removed the voting rights of most Hawaiians by restricting the vote to those with income and property. Foreign born residents, as long as they were American or European, were free to vote without proving income or property. All revenues from the Crown Lands were seized by the legislature. Since King Kalakaua was forced to sign the constitution at gunpoint, the Hawaiians referred to it as the Bayonet Constitution.

# Nine

$\mathcal{A}$round the dead man everything was moving. The leaves of the 'ulu tree clapped together in the wind, the sails of boats snapped open down at the harbor, the earth tilted and the dogs howled. The breadfruit softened in the dead man's hand. A mynah bird turned a bright eye on his shape, landing on his chest to peck at the shiny buttons of his silk shirt.

The soldiers spent several hours searching for Cornelius Rhodes, but after the commotion at the bandstand, they'd spent the rest of the afternoon hauling people off to jail. Now they were once again clustered around the dead man, asking among themselves, where was the safest place in Honolulu to hide a body until Rhodes was located?

Where had they gone last night to have a few drinks and play poker, undisturbed?

The basement of Iolani Palace.

The dead man was lifted into the back of a wagon and covered with a blanket. As the wagon moved through town, dusk seeped upward like smoke, first covering the grass and their boots, then the wagon wheels and the branches of trees, before climbing into the sky to erase the blue.

At Iolani Palace, he was carried down the dark stairwell of the servants' entrance into the basement, where he was placed on a table.

They were uneasy in the presence of the dead man and covered it with jokes. One of the soldiers put a sock on his bare foot, and another stuck a cigarette in his mouth and pretended to light it.

They wondered who he was, to cause such a commotion, and they questioned the amount of the reward. Would Rhodes pay it at all, or would he just mutter something about duty and country and keep the reward money for himself?

A wagon was sent down to the harbor for ice, and it was brought back in blocks wrapped in burlap bags. The soldiers smashed the ice with sledgehammers and took the sacks down into the basement.

The dead man was moved to a long sink in the palace kitchen, and chunks of ice were poured over him. The kitchen was crowded with objects stripped from the upstairs rooms of the palace. Tall kahilis were stuffed into the corners; feathered cloaks were dumped on the dirty floor covered in broken crockery.

A soldier who'd been rummaging through the piles of royal belongings pulled out a crown and placed it on his head. The others laughed, and the soldier took a knife and pried the jewels loose, not believing they were real. The men played a game of poker, and emeralds and rubies fell into the pockets of the young soldiers while the dead man stiffened under the ice.

That evening, Rhodes entered the basement of Iolani Palace, barely able to control his excitement. He dug the ice off the dead man's face and looked down with relief. At last, he had Kalama.

He was surprised at how fresh Kalama looked. The rope burn was fading as well. The body only needed to be hidden for a few more days.

Rhodes pulled the cigarette out of Kalama's mouth and ground it on the floor as if it were lit. He took a comb from his pocket and combed Kalama's long hair back off his forehead. The soldiers watched him, puzzled.

He caught the look on their faces and hastily put the comb away.

Feeling generous, he gave more money than he'd first promised, and after he left the palace, the soldiers celebrated with bottles of European wine they'd found in the royal pantry, toasting the dead man for the sudden good fortune he'd brought them.

*H*ow much can one country hold? By the early 1890s, Hawaii was a cup filled to the brim with disease, foreigners, guns, American Marines, religious paranoia. The sugar industry was depressed. There were frantic searches for new revenues for the kingdom. Political clubs sprouted up faster than lichens after rain. Loyalties were traded faster than the shells of hermit crabs. The secretly formed Annexation Club hoped to turn Hawaii into a territory of the United States. The Sons of Hawaii advocated the abolishment of the legislature and a full return of power to the monarchy. This was the state of the country when Lili'uokalani came to the throne in 1891, after the death of her brother Kalakaua. At that time, she was forced to swear her allegiance to the Bayonet Constitution, the very document that she believed had caused the death of her brother.

# *Ten*

$\mathcal{I}$n the dark, Eva followed McClelland down a tunnel of twisted hau trees. Faint lights were visible at the end of the path.

He pushed through a banana patch that had grown thick with neglect, and motioned her to follow.

On the other side of the trees there was a cluster of rocks circling a pool of water.

"It's hot, a thermal spring. It would be good to soak your foot in it. And my wrist."

"What happened to your wrist?"

"I believe you stepped on it," he said, and she heard the smile in his voice.

She sat down on a rock at the edge of the pool and unlaced her boots. It was quiet, and at that moment it felt like the only peaceful place left in Honolulu.

The moon disappeared behind clouds, fast as a door shutting against the light. Where was everyone hiding tonight? If the soldiers were hunting down those who were loyal to Lili'uokalani, they would need to put nearly the whole country in jail.

There was a soft murmur of water as McClelland slipped into the pool. A man that quiet was someone to be wary of. When the moon reappeared a moment later, a cloud of steam was visible rising from the surface of the pool. Eva lowered her foot into the water and quickly pulled it back out again, surprised by the heat. She thought of water bubbling up through the hot magma, finding a small vein that would push it up to the surface of the earth, to this small pond.

He turned and floated on his back, and the moonlight played over his dark shape. Eva's thoughts turned back to the dead man.

"Where have you gone?" he asked, swimming to the edge of the pool. He reached up and slowly took hold of her foot.

She was surprised, not even breathing, and he gently rotated her ankle in the water. Heat spread across the back of her neck and down her arms. She couldn't tell if it was pain or pleasure, it ran through her so quickly. He let go of her foot and the feeling disappeared. She felt herself flush and was glad that in the dark he couldn't see her face.

"I don't think anything is broken," he said. "Or else you'd be screaming right now."

"Would I?"

"No," he said, laughing. "No, I don't suppose you would."

He told her that he'd seen her yesterday at the jail. "Looking a bit stunned, you were."

"They ruined my bicycle."

"Ah, that was yours, was it?" he asked. He didn't sound surprised. "You're a seer, aren't you? Would you tell my fortune?"

Eva was at least as well known as the Chinese herbalist, or the Portuguese butcher. She was the Norwegian fortuneteller. There was no reason to be suspicious.

"So," he said. "My fortune?"

She shook her head. He didn't need his fortune told. He looked lucky, like the kind of man the world came to, rather than the other way around. Still, there was something about him, something she couldn't put her finger on, and it was probably just as well.

The banana trees rustled and an old woman stepped out between the branches. She was carrying a gun and a lantern. There were deep shadows around her eyes.

McClelland whispered to Eva that she shouldn't worry, since the gun was as old as the woman carrying it.

"You're trespassing," the woman said in a wavering voice that rose like a question.

"I'm sorry, ma'am, I didn't realize we were on private property," he said, his voice smooth and apologetic.

A man as smooth with a lie as she was. It was disconcerting to recognize your traits in someone else.

"That's you again, is it? You don't belong here. I've already warned you." The woman set the lantern down at her feet and a high green ceiling of trees flashed above them. She pointed the gun and shot just over their heads.

Eva was on her hands and knees scrambling through the bushes with no idea of direction, other than away. There was a crashing sound right next to her, and McClelland pulled her up with wet hands.

Behind them, the woman was yelling about citizenship, about the United States, about how the island was overrun with Hawaiian Royalists, all of whom needed to be shot on sight, including Queen Lili'uokalani. Especially Lili'uokalani, she yelled, and thank God the Americans have finally stepped in. They will show this country once and for all who is who.

She was still shouting as they ran through the hau trees, branches and leaves tearing at Eva's skirt and hair. When they came to a dirt road, she leaned over and tried to catch her breath.

There was dirt under her feet. She'd left her boots beside the pond, and her ankle was throbbing. She was scared and exhilarated at the same time and started laughing, and he laughed, too, a low rumbling sound.

"The Americans," he said, shaking his head. "They're even worse than the English."

"I wouldn't know," she said, pulling leaves from her hair. "I've never been to England."

"I have," he said, and left it at that.

He led the way past several empty buildings and turned up a weedy path towards a small bungalow set back off the street.

She stood on the empty lanai while he went into the house for a lamp. If you are seen entering a man's house, a voice from the past told her, your reputation will be ruined.

Too late for that, she answered.

He returned with a chair and she sat down. There was a cloth and a small brass bowl.

She took the bowl from him, and water spilled on the floor. "For your face," he explained. "I thought you were sunburnt. I didn't realize it was just dirt." He sounded amused. "I've never realized just how red the dirt here is. It seems to match your hair."

Her hands were still colored with juice from the berries, and her fingerprints bled onto the edge of the cloth.

"I was fishing," she said, suddenly confused, thinking of the frightened girl running down the beach.

She dipped the cloth in water and rubbed it across her face.

"Ah," he said, nodding. "So this is what you actually look like."

He seemed to enjoy everything, even a woman washing the dirt off her face. Why did she hold this against him? She just did. Her temper flared and then just as quickly died down.

He gave her a questioning look.

Eva stood up and tipped the water into the bushes. If I am angry, she thought, it's at myself.

She followed him into a sparsely furnished room. There was sand underfoot and she thought it odd, so far from the ocean.

He stepped over to the windows and drew the curtains shut, then lit another lamp and excused himself.

The flame flared high, and she quickly looked around, unable to hide her curiosity. There were paintings on the wall that looked like a younger version of McClelland. The same eyes, darker hair, and a slight oddness to the shape of the jaw.

He brought in a small bamboo table. He'd changed his clothes and combed his wet hair back off his face, and in the light from the lantern, she noticed a small scar below his left eye. It made her shy, as if she'd seen something she shouldn't have.

"I carry the furniture from room to room," he said, laughing. "Makes me feel like I've got a houseful of it."

He set down the table. On it was a large papaya. He cut the fruit in half and scooped out the black seeds, threw them over the edge of the lanai, and then handed half of the papaya to her.

"Here you are." It was the same uncertain voice he'd had when he offered her the berries, and for a brief moment she wanted to take his face in her hands, and then just as quickly she wanted to leave. Why you? she thought, confused. Why you and not someone else?

He was in the kitchen when she stood up and quietly moved towards the door. Her hand went out and touched the door latch. She heard him behind her and turned around. He was carrying a tray with coffee and sweet bread.

"You'll stay?" he asked, and she nodded, embarrassed.

The coffee was strong, the way she liked it.

She looked up and caught him smiling at her.

"You look like an orphan," he said, "as if someone might take your food away from you at any moment."

I don't just look like that, she thought, angry at her own vulnerability. It's what I am. For a moment she was back at the charity house her mother took her to when times were hard. There, in the company of other rough-kneed children she was constantly reminded how poor she was, and how disreputable her mother. In that place she had learned to look grateful, when what she had felt was her heart shrinking down to the size of a bitter walnut.

He doesn't know my past, she reassured herself. He just guesses well.

He held the lantern over her foot, where her anklebone had disappeared under swelling flesh. He shook his head, and a moment later he held up a bottle and two glasses.

He reminded her of the magic tricks she had learned as a child. The hat with the false bottom, the small scarf that kept unwinding. The odd smile that had you saying yes to something you didn't yet understand.

Why you, she wondered again.

He poured good rum, better than the rum Lehua and she drank late at night when they wanted to shut the window on the leper catchers, the drunken sailors, the strange cries of the 'iwa birds that haunted their neighborhood.

The drink glasses were delicate, with an etched pattern. Glasses a woman would buy, she thought.

He began speaking of his childhood, and after some time Eva relaxed enough to listen.

"We didn't have much work at home. No money, no prospects. I heard of these jobs, working in sugar cane fields, and I came here and you know, from the very first day I was paid more than the Japanese and Chinese people I worked with. Also, I wasn't indentured, like most of them. I don't know exactly what it is," he said, holding up his glass, "but sugar cane brings out the worst in people. So I quit as soon as I could afford to, started a small import shop."

He smiled and set down his glass. "The story of my life, in under two minutes."

A safe story, Eva thought. Someone else's, not his.

After a moment, he imitated the old woman with the gun. "I happen to be a citizen of the United States. . . ."

As he spoke, she stood up and set the lamp down in the middle of the room, and her shadow grew on the wall. She made two fists, pushed them together into a face with the high collar of a missionary, the chin dribbling down into the starched blade of the collar. A shadow puppet of the woman's face, her mouth moving as he spoke. "My property," he said, laughing. "Mine, mine, mine."

He moved closer to her and suddenly leaned over, his thick hair spilling forward and the back of his neck visible. Eva stared at his neck for a moment, then looked back at the wall. His hand closed to form the bill of a swan. His other hand splayed open to form wings. His fingers were long and graceful, and the wing was full. The swan glided towards the corner of the room and disappeared.

They didn't bother with trees, the palm trees that were far too easy; fir and spruce, which took a crabbier hand.

For a second the shape of the dead man floated across the wall. Eva blocked him out with the shadow of a giraffe. McClelland stood behind her and placed his hands just so to form another neck, and on the wall the necks wound around each other. She felt his breath along the back of her arm. The small lamp flickered and the animals came and went, now clear, now indistinct. An antelope with its long horns pointed towards the ceiling. Rabbits leapt through his fingers, fish swam, a fiddler crab scurried across the wall.

Soon it was hard to tell who was making which shape, and a feeling began at the back of her knees, in the place Tomas swore always itched just before a storm.

They were both laughing until he made a monkey and it was no longer funny to her.

"What?" he asked. "What is it?"

She shook her head, trying to be rid of the image that came to her, that of her mother making a fool of herself in front of small town audiences. No matter how many bonfires you made of your own past, there was no getting rid of it.

She wasn't in the habit of revealing her past to anyone, but she found herself telling him a story of her six-year-old self, a red haired girl in a red velvet dress that was a size too small the first time she wore it. A red bow in her hair. She thought she looked magnificent, like a walking fire, though no one paid her any attention. They were all too busy watching her mother. She didn't listen to her mother's words, she already knew every fortune her mother would ever tell. It was the tone she listened for, the soft exhalation that meant it was time for her to pass the hand shaped basket around the crowd, so that her mother could be paid for this thing she did, turning her skin inside out.

Next to her mother was a man playing an accordion, and he had a monkey tied to his leg on a long leash. The animal scampered through the crowd with a cup in his hand, wearing a red velvet jacket and a smart red cap with a ribbon pulled tight under his chin. He ran up to Eva and grabbed hold of the hem of her dress. It was velvet like his coat, and as soon as he touched it, he jumped on her chest and started shrieking, trying to pull her dress off her. She yelled as loudly as the monkey, and they were suddenly twirling in a circle, their teeth bared, his nails deep in her flesh, her hands around his neck.

The accordion player ran over and pulled the monkey off, and her mother glared at Eva because the crowd was no longer hers.

He took the clothes off the monkey, carefully folded the little coat, and put the hat on top of that. Then he shoved the monkey into a little box with breathing holes at the top, and the animal's little fingers reached up through the holes and clawed at the wood.

On the way home, Eva made a hundred fierce promises to herself, all of which she was too young to keep, except one. She never wore that dress again. She took it out in back of the boardinghouse and burned it with some trash, and she didn't care about the punishment she knew would follow.

When her mother discovered what she'd done with the dress, she told Eva that it wasn't the clothing that the monkey recognized. It was her.

Eva stood up, embarrassed that she'd said so much.

"Thank you," he said, looking down at his palms.

Thank you. As if she'd given him a gift.

He picked up a glass ball, rolled it back and forth across the small table. "You know, before I moved to this country I always felt that I was somewhere behind my life, running after it. My life was moving forward, without me. Now it's different. Perhaps because this is such a troubled country, but for the first time I feel like I've caught up." He looked up and smiled. "I'm moving just as fast."

Yes, Eva thought. Exactly. That is exactly what people want.

"So," McClelland said. He threw the glass ball up into the air and caught it. "I first saw glass balls on the journey here. They'd float past in the water, and at first I thought they were jellyfish, or something equally strange."

Eva nodded.

"It is amazing to think of them coming loose from the Japanese fishing nets and floating all the way here. This small glass ball, with the breath of a Japanese glassblower trapped in it. I marvel at the idea."

Eva couldn't help it, she was charmed.

He handed it to her. "You keep it," he said, and he touched her face so softly that she wondered if she'd only imagined it.

She took his hand and led him into the bedroom.

He was taller and thinner than she was, and she quickly learned the curve of bone beneath his flesh. She was falling and coming back up to the surface, diving down to the bottom of the sea, then back up to the warm water that sent its heat through her.

*The Floating City · 97*

After he fell asleep, she relit the lamp and moved through the house. There were shelves lined with bottles of fog glass, driftwood, and bits of worn seashells. Again she felt the sand underfoot, as if he'd opened a door to the sea.

Why you? she thought. Why now? Falling in love, she thought with a sudden shock. No, it was faster than falling, more like being cut by a knife. That quick, and that painful. She'd skipped the falling altogether.

She held the lantern up to the paintings she had noticed earlier. They were extraordinary. Portraits of a boy on the edge of manhood, his sweetness still visible, with eyes that looked like McClelland's but set in a rounder face.

There were more paintings in the next room. A bird she didn't recognize, perhaps a Scottish bird, just beginning to lift off the ground. A bowl of guavas so ripe she felt it in the back of her throat.

The watery bell of the milkman's horse caught her by surprise. She went back into the bedroom and looked down at McClelland's face cupped in his hand, his palm hidden, and she thought perhaps the closest intimacy of all was watching someone sleep.

She slipped the glass ball into her pocket, blew out the lamp and quietly opened the front door.

Outside, the daylight looked poured by the milkman himself, a white mist bleaching all color. A new land. The same exhilaration came over her that she had felt when she first saw this island, a sense that anything was possible.

The milkman gave a start when he saw her. "Whew, Eva. A bad morning to be out on the street. Three times already, the soldiers check my wagon. Three times I tell them it's only milk. You know what they do? They take my milk, dump it out on the road."

When Eva asked him for a ride home, he glanced at her tangled hair and ripped skirt. He patted the wooden seat and she climbed up into the cart. She was outside the rules for haole women in Honolulu.

Eva helped him deliver the milk, a bottle on each doorstep. When she was a child she would have been stealing it, not delivering. She sensed that behind a tree or hidden in the bushes, there was a hungry child, waiting.

"A fortuneteller riding a milk cart," he said. "What people think about that, eh?"

"Probably that their milk was tainted," she answered, and he laughed.

"Eh, Eva, what happens now? There are men ready to fight for the Queen. And I wonder should I go?" he said, his voice trailing off before it broke.

"I don't know," Eva answered. It's not time for you to become a hero, she thought. "You have three small children, another on the way."

He looked over at her, clearly disappointed.

At one time, she would have said anything that came into mind. People wanted to give the responsibility of their own lives to someone else, and there was more money to be made in agreeing with people than in telling them something they didn't want to hear.

And yet. Some fortuneteller she was turning out to be. She could have told him that being born into a family of fortunetellers was unlike anything else. Before you even learned to grasp a spoon, you were walking straight across a narrow board laid a foot or two above belief. Your hands were held out to the side like birds' wings, but your diaper was full. The faces you loved were at the far end of the board, their hands stretched out towards you, calling, Come, come. Already testing the limits of your childhood faith.

Eva told him about the musicians playing on the lawn of Iolani Palace, and he warned her that the new government was doing whatever it took to send people to jail. "Just for being a Royalist, eh?"

Eva nodded and said she would be more careful. But if she'd been more careful, she wouldn't have met McClelland. She reached in her pocket and touched the small sphere of glass. She felt herself absorbing everything around her: the wetness of the street, the trees rustling overhead, the morning itself, the lilting voice of the man she'd left sleeping.

"That place you picked me up," she said, trying to sound unconcerned. "What do you know about the man who lives there?"

He shrugged. "Two bottles of milk." The horse's hooves echoed on the empty street, a sound almost liquid.

"Two bottles of milk," she repeated. "What about it?"

"Plenty milk for just one man."

What did that mean? There was someone else in his life?

When the milkman dropped her off, she carried a cold bottle of milk up the steps of their lanai. She crouched down and placed it beside the door, exactly as he would have done.

She tiptoed through the house and up the stairs to bed.

Later on, Lehua would come to the front door and pick it up, and the bottle of milk would be the only thing still holding onto the coolness of morning.

*In 1893, two years after Queen Liliʻuokalani ascended the throne, she attempted to change the Bayonet Constitution with one of her own, which would reinstate the rights of native Hawaiians. The secretly formed Annexation Club, a group of men consisting of haole politicians, foreigners, and missionary descendants, saw Liliʻuokalani's constitution as an act of treason. They quickly renamed themselves the Committee of Safety, and with the help of a boatload of American Marines, took over the government buildings and dismantled the Hawaiian military. The Queen abdicated only under protest, hoping to avoid bloodshed and believing that the United States would soon help to restore her kingdom. Meanwhile, the Committee of Safety moved into Iolani Palace, which they established as their headquarters. They ordered everything stripped from the palace walls —paintings of Hawaiian kings and queens, the feather kahilis that signified royalty, all of it was dumped in the basement. The Committee of Safety, most of whom had arrived in Hawaii worth less than the barnacles on the bottom of a boat, now walked through the empty rooms of the palace marveling at their good fortune, seeing themselves as the culmination of Western expansion, like the last of the whalers, aiming their harpoons at this land that dared rise above the sea and show itself. An entire country, theirs for the taking.*

# Eleven

As the sun was rising on the windward side of the island and Honolulu still crouched in darkness, Eva dreamt of the woman who had died on the boat. In the dream it was the day of the woman's funeral, and Eva watched her falling through the ocean, only she was there with her in the water, the two of them synchronized, twirling around each other, their hands splayed open like starfish. The dead woman grabbed Eva's wrist and started pulling her to the bottom of the sea.

Lehua shook her awake. "I hea 'oe i hele maewa aku nei?" she asked softly. Where did you go wandering?

Eva closed her eyes. If you didn't see a nightmare through to the very end, you'd never be rid of it.

Lehua's fingers were drops of water tapping her skin. "Eva. Why are you still sleeping?"

Eva groaned and sat up in a tangle of sheets.

"You were making such strange noises. What were you dreaming?"

"Water," she answered, kicking her legs free of the sheet. "The sea."

She sat up, and Lehua handed her a cup of the green tea that smelled like trampled grass. She opened the newspaper and spread it across Eva's lap.

Lehua pointed to an article on the second page. "Read this."

The body of a man had been found in the canal that ran along the back of Waikiki. The approximate age was given, and hair color. There wasn't much else said, not even his race. Especially not his race.

"Do you think it is the same man?"

"No, they don't even know where his body is."

Lehua nodded in agreement. "You know what I think?" she asked excitedly. "No one was found in the canal in Waikiki. They're lying."

"Why do you say that?" Eva asked.

"Because they're haole."

"But I'm haole."

"At least you aren't American," Lehua said, "even if you do lie all the time."

"There's more than one kind of lying," Eva protested. "Besides, it's how I make my living."

Eva read to the end of the article, where there was a notice that anyone who could identify him should report to the police station. She shook her head. "And get themselves into trouble."

There was a knocking at the front door, and Lehua went downstairs.

Eva lifted the sheet like a sail over her body and let it fall. First it touched the tips of her toes, her face, then her knees, breasts, shoulders. McClelland, she thought, as the cool fabric settled over her skin.

She wanted to tell Lehua about him, but she was cautious of jinxing happiness by putting it into words.

Downstairs, voices of American tourists mingled with Lehua's. If Lehua was in a good mood, she taught them how to say good morning in Hawaiian, or to ask how much something cost. If she was in a bad mood, she taught them how to tell people they looked like death, or that they wouldn't let a pig wear that hat.

The tourists couldn't understand that no matter how much money they spent, they were still unpopular with the street vendors.

Eva picked up the newspaper and ripped out the article about the dead man. She smoothed out the edges of the paper, concentrating on the man, on what had happened that day on the beach. The only image that came to her was a pattern of cranes flying across long gold sleeves. A kimono. A woman's kimono.

When Eva concentrated on Queen Lili'uokalani, she saw her surrounded by wooden boxes. She couldn't make sense of the image. What would she be packing? Where would she be going? Queen Lili'uokalani would never abandon her own country.

As she dressed, what came to her were all the signs she had read incorrectly. You'll be safe on that boat, Eva had told more than one young sailor, now drowned. She'd seen visions of bloody knives in the hands of schoolboys, with no idea that they'd wind up behind the counter at the butcher shop rather than in prison for murder.

She glanced in the mirror, noticing that her clothing hung loose on her frame. When had she become so thin? Her hipbones pushed forward, and her belly curved inward like a caldera. She remembered another woman, much thinner than herself, standing at the bottom of the stairs in Oslo.

She turned away from the mirror, pulled out her paints and brushes and a stack of thick white paper that she used for painting tarot cards. It was Eva and her grandmother who painted the cards. Her mother implied that this was beneath her, and said it was like revisiting your nightmares. But to Eva, the cards weren't nightmares, they were explanations. She reached for a blank card and picked up a brush. This one would be for her mother.

She decided to begin with the thin woman and paint what looked like snow falling out of her mouth.

She set the paintbrush down and rubbed her eyes, remembering standing at the top of the stairs at the boardinghouse in Oslo. She hadn't expected that her mother's lover would be there as well.

He held a small silk purse in his hand, the one her mother kept her money in.

They argued, and then his hand flashed out and clutched her shoulder bone, his fingers digging into the tendons.

Eva grabbed onto the banister and twisted her body, trying to break his painful grip.

The landlady came into view at the bottom of the long stairs, and she stared up at them, wondering. His fingers dug farther into Eva's shoulder, but she finally pulled loose.

They were both suddenly off balance and then he was falling, but falling slowly, arms out to the sides the way circus performers did, just before they pulled themselves back up, saved with ropes and nets.

He tumbled down the stairs. Even then Eva expected him to stand up, dust off his trousers, take a small bow. But he didn't move. The landlady looked from him to Eva and back to him. Eva kept her eyes on the woman's face, not wanting to see his crumpled shape.

The landlady had been in the kitchen eating cookies when the argument started, and her mouth was still ringed in powdered sugar. "Go," she said. "Run away. While you can." As she spoke, the powdered sugar fell from her lips down across the front of her dress. As if her mouth were snowing.

"But I did nothing wrong," Eva said. She couldn't move, she didn't want to come down the stairs, she didn't want to be near the body of her mother's lover. "I didn't push him. He fell on his own."

"Your mother will never believe you." The woman took a step

closer to the body and looked down. "She'll never forgive you, either. She had hopes for this one."

"He was stealing her money," Eva protested.

The landlady sighed. "Which of them haven't? Take a train," she said, "whatever train is leaving."

It took a disaster for Eva to realize how much she wanted to be gone from that life. She ran back to her mother's room, found Mormor's black suitcase filled with paints and brushes. On the dresser was the deck of her handpainted tarot cards.

She didn't head in the direction of the train station. She knew the landlady would tell her mother, who would send the police after her. Instead, she ran towards the harbor. A train was easily traceable, with the police waiting at the next stop, but anyone could get lost on the water.

Yet, on the long voyage to Hawaii, he was there in the heave of the boat, in the hot still days, in the very smell of the hard biscuits she ate to fight seasickness. He followed her all the way to Honolulu. She saw him in a stranger's gesture, in a tree's shadow, and for a split second, she saw him in the dead man they'd found that day on the beach.

She picked up a smaller brush, and painted the snow falling from the woman's mouth, building into a drift at her feet.

Sugar.


*T*he afternoon brought a knock on the door, and Eva pretended that she wasn't hoping it would be McClelland, that she wasn't thinking of him at all.

The man at the door wore an entirely blank face, making her more cautious than if he'd been wearing a policeman's uniform. There was another man standing behind him.

They asked for Eva Hanson.

"She's not here," Eva said.

"We'd like to come inside, Miss Hanson."

"No, I don't think that's possible," she answered, but he had already wedged the tip of his boot in the doorframe.

They pushed the door open, entered the kitchen, and glanced around.

The blank-faced man told Eva that his orders were to confiscate the bottles of pills she'd been selling.

"Why?" she asked, startled.

"You are making false claims, and that's illegal."

"And who decides that?" she asked, though she already knew the answer. They would do whatever Cornelius Rhodes ordered.

"People are being arrested, Miss Hanson. I'd think you'd be willing to cooperate. You're getting off easy."

No, Eva thought, I am being singled out. The thought panicked her.

"I have a list of people who were at yesterday's demonstration at the palace."

"It was a concert."

He took a step closer. "Don't feign ignorance, Miss Hanson. It was a gathering of Royalists."

This isn't about Royalists or sugar pills, Eva thought, it's about the dead man. It was suddenly confusing. Which dead man were they concerned with, the one on the other side of the world, or the one here?

He pointed to the bottles lined up on the counter.

"Get rid of them," he told the other man, who swept the bottles off the counter, smashing the thin glass with the heel of his boot. Colored pills scattered in all directions.

Eva pushed herself against the wall, willing herself not to show alarm.

They broke every single bottle, even those that were empty. The blank-faced man came closer and wiped his open palm across her chest. They stared at each other until he finally pulled away.

"You need to clean up this mess," he said.

Eva crouched down and began cleaning up the glass and colored pills flattened into the wood. Shards of glass had to be pried up with a knife. She didn't look up until she heard the door slam shut. She wept softly as she scraped the floor.

That afternoon, she did everything twice. She took off the clothes she'd been wearing and put on clean clothes, but she still felt the hot imprint of the man's hand on her chest, and so changed again. She washed the dishes twice, she swept the lanai twice. The handle of the broom had a picture glued around it of a Hawaiian girl in a hula skirt who was also holding a broom. She peeled the label off and looked at it closely. Where was she now, the girl who had posed for this illustration of what a happy Hawaiian woman was supposed to look like?

She took out the newspaper article about the dead man and reread it, wondering why they insisted on connecting him to her. She worried over the kimono with the pattern of flying cranes.

Folding the article in half, she placed it in the box with the jade necklace. As an afterthought, she added the sweeping hula girl, and then hid the box in a new place. She knew that from this point forward, everything she did would somehow be used against her.


*T*he weather hissed, sent wild itching heat around her legs, left her with half a brain as soon as she was out on the hot street. Noisy mynah birds strutted across the road, their feathers black as a missionary's coat. Palm trees scratched themselves in the wind, and dark skinned women made promises to men passing on the street, their bright tongues flashing like the pink coin in a chameleon's neck.

Trees threw down the shadows of animals, and Eva thought of McClelland's hands. She felt herself pulled towards him like a fish on a very long line. A fish that hadn't yet felt the hook.

Carriages passed by, and in the heat the horses seemed to be swimming. A group of women sat in a doorway, sharing the same fan, listening to a man with a ukulele playing one of the Queen's songs. Eva tossed a coin into the small hat at his feet. Then he played a favorite song of the haole politicians, and she was not the only one who turned away.

She took a shortcut through an alley of busy coffin-builders, men whose grandfathers had built fine boats for Kamehameha the Great but were now busy hammering together coffins for Hawaiians, who were dying faster than they were being born. The missionaries called it God's will, but there were other names for it: measles, cholera, venereal disease, leprosy.

Building coffins was the steadiest job in town.

Freshly cut planks were propped against the wall. Eva stopped and ran her hand over the wood. Her grandmother's coffin had been the least expensive, plain pine. Her funeral had been attended by other fortunetellers, as well as circus acrobats, musicians, and anyone else who had a thirst for free drink.

A carpenter stepped through a doorway with a small coffin in his hands. He leaned it up against the wall and wrote a name on it with a piece of chalk, and Eva quickly turned away.

At the corner, a half-empty tram clattered past. Cornelius Rhodes sat in the front seat, his face filling an entire window. Eva pulled back into the crowd so he wouldn't see her. A moment later, she wasn't certain that she'd seen him at all. The town was full of men with large pink faces, and perhaps she was simply unnerved by the heat.

Up ahead, a laughing crowd stared at an elaborately carved sign hanging under the rafters. It was splattered in black paint, and a small pool of paint dripped down onto the sidewalk.

"Again and again this shop sign gets painted," a man said.

"Whose shop is it?" Eva asked.

"Opium dealers."

"It must be expensive, replacing the sign."

"Not if you're selling opium."

Eva turned down towards the harbor and the large wooden

warehouse that held the fishing supply store, which sold every-thing from dungarees to wooden getas, from fans of split bam-boo to bicycles.

The worn door was propped open with a large coralhead, and the wind moved a salty paw across the bolts of sailcloth, the sex-tants and barrels of tar. Eva ran her palms over the coils of rope, the dark sailor's caps, the buckets of loose nails.

The counters were buried under the bolts of cloth that the missionaries favored, a thick fabric that was harsh against the skin. The missionaries had instructed Hawaiian women to sew the fabric into long dresses that were entirely unsuitable for the tropics. The women were given scissors and told holo, which meant start, and they cut the fabric until they heard ku, which meant stop, which meant that enough fabric had been cut to cover their bodies from head to toe. The dresses were called holoku. The Hawaiians called it a start-stop dress, joking that the missionaries were now even telling people's clothing what to do.

At the back of the shop, the old sailors still played cards like men out at sea: endless time combined with limited space. Their movements were slight and close to the body, their hands bar-nacled with age, and the game had been going on for as long as anyone cared to remember.

A Hawaiian man stepped back from the counter so that Eva would be waited on first. She shook her head, and motioned him forward. Haoles were always served before Hawaiians, and Hawaiians before Pakes, the Chinese.

A young clerk told her there were no bicycles in stock, his voice dipping and rising like a bird fishing out at sea. He was Swedish, and Eva switched from English to Norwegian. As they spoke, she thought they sounded like two last species, on the verge of extinction.

Behind him was a locked case crowded with sextants, each one gleaming bright as a bicycle wheel.

"Ah, you know what the boats are like. The next shipment could take weeks, could take months. Unless the boat sinks. Then never, of course," he added, smiling at the thought.

As Eva wrote her name down on what the clerk jokingly called a wish list rather than a waiting list, she planned her next tarot card: the ocean floor littered with drowned bicycles, small tattooed fish swimming between barnacle encrusted spokes. What would it mean? You have lost your way, the journey you chose wasn't yours to follow.

She bought another case of glass bottles for her pills. She wasn't about to let anyone stop her from making a living.

*On* the way home, she decided to visit McClelland. She changed directions, heading down the dirt road to his cottage.

A large jacaranda tree shaded the roof, something she hadn't noticed last night. This morning, she corrected herself, feeling both pleased and flustered, as if parts of herself that had never met were finally coming together.

She walked up a path littered with lavender petals, took a deep breath, and then knocked on a door painted the dark blue color of deep water.

There was no answer.

The door wasn't locked. She smoothed down her hair and slipped into the room. For a moment it felt like the wrong house, but the few rickety pieces of bamboo furniture were still in place. Against the far wall was where his wrist had formed the neck of a swan.

Yet the house felt abandoned, like a circus grounds after the performance, when there was nothing left but indentations in the grass, the holes for the wooden spikes the only proof that just the night before that spot had held up a magnificent tent.

He had never told her he was leaving.

She glanced through the empty room. Part of her had once

admired any disappearance. Another part still expected it. Why should he be any different? She pushed her forehead against the wall, heard her breath coming from somewhere outside herself.

She wouldn't go into his bedroom, search the tall wardrobe against the wall that she already knew was empty. She thought of the glass ball he'd given her, sitting on her bedside table. Her face flushed, and she kicked over a bamboo table, making it slide across the floor. No one should trick a trickster, she thought. Never.

Mormor used to say that men were two-thirds water, that they slipped through your fingers and took part of you with them. She wondered what she could have been thinking. That she could ruin her mother's happiness and still expect it for herself?

She was tempted to find the house where the old woman with the gun lived. Perhaps he went back to her thermal pool and this time she took proper aim. But someone who shot above his head one night wasn't likely to shoot through his heart the following day.

In the front yard, she tore a plumeria from a branch and swore that one day she would meet a man who was less of a charlatan. Someone less like herself.

There was a man staring at her through the hedge, his dark face bobbing among the leaves.

She asked if he had seen McClelland. Her voice was high and thin and peculiar sounding.

The man said that the tall haole man was gone. He pointed up towards the mountain. "Went mauka."

"Was anyone with him?" she asked, humiliated by her question and yet holding out a faint hope that he was simply in trouble. At least then it wouldn't be another woman.

"Nah, he was alone. Took a lot of things with him."

"What sort of things?"

The man shrugged. She'd asked too many wrong questions.

"It is McClelland you're talking about?" she asked.

"Calls himself MacEnulty."

This much she suddenly knew, hearing the Mac. People who switched names needed to keep a part of the last one, like a sore tooth that they continue to favor. Sometimes pain is as hard to give up as pleasure.

She walked quickly down the street, kicking at leaves and twigs and anything else in her path. She wasn't angry, angry would have been far easier. She was devastated.

She reminded herself that she should have been more careful, that he was a stranger. Yet they were all strangers here, weren't they?

*A*fter Queen Liliʻuokalani's forced abdication in 1893, photographs of the Committee of Safety, now calling itself the Provisional Government, quickly flooded Honolulu. The shop windows were so crowded with the white faces of the new government that a joke circulated that the photographs had all been taken before the overthrow of the monarchy, not after.

Their expressions were studious, but what of all the frippery covering their chests? The bows and rows of medals lined up like ribbon candy, where were those so quickly found? These men couldn't point to a medal and say, I won this one in a war. None of them had been to war, none had seen active service. There was barely a scratch to show for the overthrow of a country.

They modeled themselves on the leaders of the French Revolution, a parallel that quickly dissolved when it was pointed out that Hawaii wasn't their country to begin with. Still, the photographs were handed out as gifts and souvenirs, the way the Hawaiian flag had been taken down and cut into small pieces and offered to a crowd of white faces while the American flag was raised in its place.

# Twelve

*W*hen dusk fell, Eva was still sitting in the same chair, trying to see a pattern in the whirlwind of the last few days. Instead of answers, what came to her were simply the things of night: roaches, mosquitoes, moths tapping against the other side of the glass.

A light rain started and just as quickly stopped and she could see no sense to any of it. A man who had disappeared, a scared politician, and a policeman under his control. And all of them expecting something from her.

She had miscalculated, she was no better a judge of people than her own mother. Look where it had gotten her. McClelland was probably even now speaking of her, bragging about what had occurred between them, the way her mother's lovers always did.

She held her hands out in front of her. When had they stopped looking like her hands? She stood up and blew a breath to fog the window. So who was she now?

She wondered if it would be possible to leave the business of fortunetelling behind her, find some other way to make a living that was of less interest to the police.

A seamstress? She hated to sew. A governess? She was too poorly educated, and the sort of knowledge she did have wasn't what parents wanted their children learning. A prostitute? Never entertained the thought. A pickpocket, once again? Tempting as always, and Eva did possess hands of poured oil, but Honolulu was too small a town for that.

Fortunetelling was what she was trained to do, it was all the women in her family had ever done, regardless of whether they possessed the gift of clairvoyance. For Eva, the future had been decided on a night when she was six years old.

Instead of bedtime stories, her mother would read aloud the crime pages of the newspaper, followed by the obituaries. For young Eva, these were tales that kept her awake and terrified. On that night, Eva's mother read her an article about a husband who had burned to death in a house fire, leaving behind a heart-broken widow.

Her mother folded the newspaper in half, and half again, wondering how much money the widow would receive; if it were a sufficient amount, then the poor woman would certainly be in need of their services. Giving comfort to the bereaved was a lucrative business for more than ministers and undertakers, and fortunetellers had the added lure of being able to contact the dead.

Eva sat up in her bed. "That man died before the house caught fire," she said.

Her mother's face came so close to hers that fine lines were visible across her pale skin, light as bird tracks over snow. "What do you mean, the man died before the fire?" she asked.

"Nothing," Eva said, distrusting her mother's expression. "I meant nothing by it."

Yet she had always been able to see who was unhappy, who had done something so wrong that he was permanently altered by it. She could spot a broken heart, a crack in the soul. Those people were as obvious to her as if their faces were painted bright green, but until that moment it was something she'd kept to herself. Hadn't Mormor told her that all gifts punish their owner, especially in a family like theirs?

"Tell me what you saw."

Eva closed her eyes.

Her mother tapped the back of her hand with a sharp fingernail. "Tell me."

"Someone set him on fire after he was already dead and then later burned the house down."

"Who set him on fire?" her mother asked, in the tone of voice that calls one sort of child away from the edge of a cliff and sends another over. The last thing she wanted was her own child pulling off her hard-earned cloak of illusion.

Over time, Eva had carefully watched her mother's pretended possession of the spirit and subsequent fainting spells, and she had learned that the point of their act was artifice itself. They were the wink at the end of the joke.

Her mother questioned her again, and Eva shook her head. She hadn't seen everything, just that one image. The dead man lying on his bed, then the bed doused with liquid and a match set to it.

Several days later, the newspapers reported that the young widow had broken down and confessed to murder. Eva's mother looked at her thoughtfully.

Now here she was, still in the same business. She could offer the excuse that it was all she knew, but the truth was far simpler. It was hard to let go of something she was good at.

*W*hen she had first settled in Honolulu, Eva put weekly notices in the newspapers, alongside those of the other fortune-tellers and spiritualists in town. Eva's claims were more modest than those of her competition. She hinted at the possibility of happiness. Of satisfaction. When few responded in those first weeks, she added communication with the dead, and business quickly picked up.

For some, a visit to the fortuneteller was like going to confession. People gave a glimpse of their hearts to a total stranger and then walked away from it, feeling that some weight had been taken off. Eva's job was that of the stranger.

She received her customers in a small room with a discreet entrance at the back of Lehua's house. After all, peering into a person's life was an embarrassing business. What did they come to her for? Mostly for reassurances over love affairs, though Eva had found the odds to be better in poker than in love.

The room was cluttered with candles, small silver spheres, and a red silk tablecloth, but she might as well have a coral head to read, a spill of sand, the long thin needle of a palm leaf. The eye of a mynah bird. Any props would do.

Tonight, a Kona wind began, bringing the sound of horses, men's voices, and the creaking of wagon wheels. Eva quickly blew out the lamp and sat in the dark, listening.

There was a soft knock on the door, and a low whistle that Eva recognized as that of her neighbor, the Widow.

She pulled her into the room and quickly locked the door behind her.

"Did you hear the wagon? Soldiers," the Widow said, pulling her shawl closer. "Coming and going like this in the middle of the night, it's no good."

Eva fumbled for the matches and relit the lamp. "What do you think they're doing?"

"No idea. Listen, Eva. The police come by, ask questions."

"Questions about me?" she asked nervously.

The Widow leaned forward, and patted her cheek. "I tell them nothing."

Eva stood up and put the kettle on for tea, trying to keep her nervousness in check, her hands occupied. She set out two cups and a loaf of sweet bread.

The Widow finally spoke. "You know, every year I wait for a good flower for the orchid show. Some orchids take their time. Take years." She slapped her hand down on the table, startling Eva.

"I feel like one of those missionaries, waiting for their God to show up. What can they do to hurry Him up? Nothing. Just wait. In this town we are all waiting, eh?"

*Q*ueen Lili'uokalani actively petitioned the United States government for help in reestablishing her monarchy. Several months after the Queen's abdication, President Cleveland sent an emissary to Hawaii to discover the reasons for the overthrow of the monarchy.

The emissary, James Blount, concluded that the Provisional Government's claim that American lives and property were in danger was completely false, and that the United States Marines had acted illegally. The Provisional Government's members were not revolutionaries, as they claimed to be, but mere adventurers. He strongly recommended an immediate return of the monarchy to Queen Lili'uokalani.

The Provisional Government refused to yield, even going to the point of sandbagging the palace, in case the American government should attempt to use force against them.

The matter was sent to the U.S. Congress, but by this time expansionist views were again popular. Not wanting to go to war against United States citizens, the Senate voted against the monarchy.

# Thirteen

$\mathcal{B}$y the next morning, word had spread that the soldiers had been through the neighborhood during the night, and Lehua decided to hide her belongings under the house.

In the back garden, she crouched down and handed wrapped bundles to Malia, who scrambled under the house with them. Around the two figures, the chickens raced through the long grass, turning it into a mad sea.

Eva watched for a moment before clearing her throat. They looked up with startled faces.

"Lehua is hiding everything," Malia said excitedly, "before the soldiers steal it."

Lehua nodded, agreeing. "The police are bad enough. Now the soldiers are searching houses for guns, and they're keeping anything they find. Silver, money. This morning the Widow saw two soldiers carrying a desk out of someone's house."

"How can they do that?" Malia asked.

Lehua shrugged. "They do what they want."

Eva watched Lehua carefully, checking for signs of the depression that always led to an opium pipe. She's doing better today, Eva reassured herself. This is simply about soldiers, nothing more. And for Malia it is a game.

"The Republic's men are still watching the Queen," Lehua said. "They hide behind her gardenia hedge smoking so many cigarettes that it looks like the bushes are on fire."

Eva shook her head.

"I want to hide this," Malia said, pulling a small pink stone from her pocket.

"Best to be safe," Eva agreed, thinking that childhood was a walk over a precarious bridge and not everyone made it across intact.

"And this." Malia held up a sketch of a humpback whale drawn in Tomas's spidery hand. He had taught Malia to draw, and now the child drew everything with the same shaky hand.

"Shall we hide this?" Eva teased, handing her a bright satin ribbon the color of egg yolks.

Eva tied the end of the ribbon around the child's waist, and Malia twirled in the grass. The top of her head smelled sweet and a little burnt, like toffee mixed with dirt.

Keiki o ka aina, Lehua called her. A child of the land.

Malia peeled the petals off a hibiscus flower and pulled out the small hidden cone at the flower's center. She stuck it on the end of her nose. "This is how sea monsters look," she informed them.

Eva hugged Malia quickly. "Frightening," she whispered.

Lehua gestured towards a large pile of neatly wrapped bundles. One was clearly a gun, wrapped in oil-soaked rags. "You have anything you want hidden?"

Eva thought of the jade necklace. Or perhaps the glass ball that McClelland had given her. "Nothing," she said.

Lehua looked at her curiously. "Well, fine. But who knows what those pupule haoles will do next," she warned.

Malia nodded in agreement. Crazy white people were unpredictable. Eva suspected that they placed her in that category as well.

Lehua mentioned that the Widow's nephew was still missing, though there was a rumor that the police had taken him into custody. Upon hearing this, the Widow went downtown and threatened the police with her machete. "Lucky for them she didn't have any black paint with her, or she would have doused the whole building," Lehua added.

"What happened to her?"

"They brought her home. They took away her machete, though. She's still upset."

"I'll get her another one," Eva said.

She wondered if McClelland's name was on the lists of the missing. No, it was more likely that she'd see him walking down the street with a wife on his arm, and what would she do then? Her fingers pressed small nervous pleats into the fabric of her skirt.

"What do you think will happen next?" Lehua asked.

"I don't know," Eva answered. "I try to see something, anything, but there are only small glimpses."

Lehua wiped her face with the back of her arm and her damp skin glistened, and Eva thought of something the Widow had told her.

Because Lehua was hapa-haole, half Hawaiian and half white, the missionaries saw her color as a visible sin, a mixing of the races, and they shunned her. Even her haole father had taught in a school his own child wasn't allowed to attend. He spent each day teaching white children, and at night he would come home and rub a special bleaching cream into her skin. He claimed it was only the sun that turned her skin brown, rather than the fact that he had married a Hawaiian woman, and she understood that his relationship with her mother was an unfortunate, momentary weakness. Eventually, he left her at the orphanage across the street and moved back to the United States. There, he started another family. Haole, this time.

The Widow suspected that like Malia, Lehua was still waiting for her father to come back to her. She said that she personally hoped the man rotted in hell.

"Here's a note we got this morning," Lehua said, pulling an envelope from her pocket. "I found it slipped under the front door, like all the others."

It was one of many anonymous notes Eva had received. For a moment, Eva saw Rhodes frowning from the tram window. He was the sort of man who would send anonymous notes.

"Free publicity," Eva said, trying not to show how much the note worried her.

The mood in Honolulu was changing. Even the Widow, that black clothed barometer, now kept a long hunting knife under her bed. Right here, she had told Eva, tapping the base of her throat. This is the place where you kill someone, fast.

Eva decided to keep the gun. She took it off the top of the pile and set it aside.

Lehua watched her, saying nothing.

Eva reread the note.

The last note had had to do with the fact that she never went to church. They were lucky that she didn't. Her mother used to attend church dressed as a wealthy widow, and when the collection plate passed by she'd lean forward and, with her veil hiding her hands, she'd drop in one bill and lift out five.

This note was more malevolent, suggesting that it would be better for everyone if she no longer lived on the island. She was, as a white woman, a bad example to the community. Like the previous notes, this one was written in block letters.

Lehua reminded Eva that the card game at Lili'uokalani's house was this afternoon. At the back door, she stepped into a bucket of water and scrubbed the dirt off her feet, pulled her dark hair into a bun, and stuck a chopstick through it.

In the kitchen, she unwrapped a package of meat. "I am cooking up all the food that will go bad, and hiding everything else."

Eva wondered if everyone prepared for war in such an odd way. What should the old sailors next door do? Bury their scrimshaw? Buy more potatoes? Sharpen the blades on knives as brittle as their old bones?

She stared at the trail of Lehua's wet footprints and decided to do what she always did in times of crisis. Find a way to make money out of the confusion.

Lehua's bare feet brushed against the kitchen floor, moving back and forth with the sound of something being erased. Eva watched her for a moment and then leaned down, lit the stove, and dropped the note onto the flames.


$\mathcal{T}$hat afternoon, Eva and Lehua were invited to a card game at the Queen's private home. They walked between the fruit trees, and ferns in large porcelain containers. Lehua told her that the house had once belonged to Lili'uokalani's haole mother-in-law, a woman who never forgave her son for marrying a Hawaiian woman, even if she was royalty.

At the front door, Lehua put her hand up to the knocker and glanced over at Eva. "Don't cheat," she said, under her breath.

Eva tried to look insulted. "I would never," she answered.

Lehua laughed as she knocked on the door.

The large living room was filled with tables, women moving chairs and plumping pillows. There was a deck of new cards on every table.

The small room off the living room was draped in the women's jackets, shawls, and purses. In the living room, tea was being served. Eva picked up a small crocheted purse, rubbing her fingers across the nubby surface. She set it down, chose another purse, and snapped it open. A handkerchief, a bottle of pills, and small change.

What is wrong with these women, Eva wondered. She glanced at the door, then opened another purse, which held a small Bible and folded money. Eva plucked out a bill, folded it into her pocket, and turned just as Lehua came through the door with a cup of tea.

She glanced at Eva, then down at the purses.

"Is that my tea?" Eva asked.

Lehua shook her head and walked back into the living room. Eva followed.

Eva sat down, feeling awkward in the dress she'd borrowed from Lehua. She watched the women attempting to shuffle the new decks of cards, as if trying to stack blocks of wood. She had to resist the impulse to take the cards from them and do a proper job of it. They all played intently, and badly.

The games were short and the women changed tables often. Eva played twice at the Queen's table. She glanced about, trying to see in their faces who might be the one sending her threatening notes. After a moment, they all looked guilty.

After several more games, the Queen remarked that Eva was successful at every table but hers.

"One never knows how games of chance will go, Your Highness."

"Ah, but it is my understanding that people in your profession know exactly how chance will go," Lili'uokalani answered, smiling.

*T*he Provisional Government declared itself the Republic of Hawaii on July 4, 1894. One of their members, Sanford Dole, elected himself president of the Republic. They unveiled a new constitution, which declared that in order to vote people must be able to speak, read, and write in English, thereby successfully excluding the majority of Japanese, Chinese, and Hawaiians from having a say in the government.

People questioned how such a thing had come to pass. Some said the trouble started back with the Bayonet Constitution. Others said the troubles began much further back, with the arrival of the missionaries in 1820. Back then, the Hawaiians had listened to the missionaries' stories with interest and eventually with affection, in that way people have of mistaking the teller for the tale and so fall in love with both.

# *Fourteen*

The women in Eva's family had always been fluent in the language of the lifted wallet, the sharp blade hissing through the bottom of a purse, the exchange of bills, the slight curving movement of the hand used to warn each other of danger.

Tonight, she wasn't surprised to see her hand pull itself into that same warning shape, here on the other side of the world. The last thing she wanted to do was to go out into Honolulu, and yet she didn't feel safe staying at home. But she had a job this evening, a steady client she didn't want to lose.

On the way out, she latched the windows and locked the door behind her, not knowing if she was locking Jonathan in or out, and not caring. When the neighborhood dogs barked, she looked to see if anyone was watching from the street, and the shapes of men in black suits filled every shadow.

It was a windy night, and Eva stayed off the busy streets, choosing instead the footpaths and alleys behind the small shops. She tried to convince herself that she wasn't depressed over McClelland, but at the same time she could barely wait to close her eyes on the day.

She arrived at the house of Mrs. Yascovitch, a respectable

woman who couldn't afford to be seen going to a fortuneteller, and so instead Eva came to her, in the middle of the night.

Mrs. Yascovitch invited her in, offering a chair. Eva sat down and watched the woman grip the edges of her own chair and gingerly lower herself into the seat as someone would lower herself into a hot bath.

She was the wife of a Russian sailor who'd been lost at sea. Lost at sea was a common euphemism in Honolulu, a way of explaining any disappearance, though in this case it was true.

She poured Eva a cup of the tea neither of them ever drank. As she leaned forward and handed her the cup, Eva smelled lavender. Eva saw her ironing her best blouse, slipping it on while it was still warm, and then applying a drop of lavender water to the inside of her wrists, where the bones were delicate as shells.

She was still pining for her husband.

Eva shuffled the cards and fanned them out across the table. Mrs. Yascovitch hesitated a moment, then chose her first card. Eva turned it over. The card was of disaster, a bird falling through the sky. Mrs. Yascovitch's eyes were weak, thank God. Eva tapped the card. "Good," she said.

She picked the rest of the cards, and Eva nodded at each choice. "This is very clear," she said. "A man who wants you to know that he still loves you."

Mrs. Yascovitch flushed, nervously opening and closing her locket, with the small steady rap of gunfire.

"He misses you," Eva continued, pointing at another card. "He misses your . . . ah, physical self."

She turned even redder.

"He wants you to pick the first flower you see and place it behind your ear."

Mrs. Yascovitch leaned back from the table. "I couldn't possibly do that."

For a moment it was quiet enough to hear the water chasing over the rocks in the stream that ran alongside her house.

Eva wondered if she'd gone too far. There were always those who resisted what they desired most, especially in matters of love.

Mrs. Yascovitch touched her throat. "Anything else?" she whispered.

"No, I'm sorry. That's all the cards are telling me this evening."

She paid twice the usual amount. Eva buttoned her coat against the rain, and as the older woman's door closed and locked behind her, Eva imagined her waking up tomorrow morning, walking through her garden, her hand hovering like a hummingbird above the bright red flower.

Eva had no idea whether or not she would pick it. Sometimes it was best not to know what happens next.

The streets were empty due to the rain, and on the way home she noticed a light coming from Edward's office.

She tried the door, surprised to find it unlocked. She quietly let herself in. The outer room was empty, but she could hear Edward arguing with someone in his office.

"He was supposed to take care of that," he said.

"Well, clearly he didn't," someone answered angrily.

Chairs scraped the floor. They were standing up.

Eva quietly left the building and raced across the street, wedging herself into the shadow between two shops. The man came out the door of Edward's office. His umbrella hid his face, but he had the self-assured walk of a politician.

She crossed the street a moment later. The door was still unlocked and Eva let herself in.

Edward was startled to see her. "Whew, you gave me a scare. It's the middle of the night, Eva. What on earth are you doing here?"

"You should lock your doors, Edward."

"So I should. Especially on a night that would bring you here," he joked.

"I was just passing by."

"Sure you were," he said.

"May I sit down?"

He waved towards a chair, then opened a desk drawer and pulled out a bottle of rum and held up two glasses.

She nodded.

He poured them both a shot, and drank his down at once. "Needed that," he said, putting the bottle away. "So, what brings you out on such a windy night?"

McClelland's face floated past, and she took a sip of rum.

"Eva, I asked you a question."

She looked up, startled. Edward was staring at her.

"Well," she said, deciding not to mention the argument she had just heard.

"Well, what?" he asked impatiently.

"I just want to know if you've found out anything," she said, nervously fingering her skirt.

"Listen, Eva. Whatever this is you are involved in, I don't want to be connected."

"Involved in?"

"Eva, you can't afford it, and neither can I." He took out his pocket watch and opened it, and the blur of a woman's face appeared and disappeared. "I have plans. And I will not have them jeopardized by you or anyone else."

"Edward. I just need to know what you've found out."

"What makes you think I know anything at all?"

"Look at yourself. How you are acting."

"You're one to talk," he said. He stepped around behind his desk and unlocked a drawer. He held up a wallet. "You know, I have enough money for you to purchase a boat fare away from here."

Edward was turning into someone she'd rather steal from than accept money from. "I like living here," she said.

"You and me," Edward said. "What does it matter to us, this island?" He picked up his fountain pen and pointed it at Eva. "We were once a great deal alike, Eva. Let me give you some advice. It's time for a fresh start."

No, Eva thought. We were once alike, but not now. I still steal my money and you plan to marry yours. "Am I to assume that your attempts to marry the daughter of a wealthy missionary aren't working?"

"Win some, lose some." He pulled out the bottle and poured another shot. "I've already had to cross three names off my list," he confessed. "Listen. I'll tell you what I've heard, and it's not good. The man you found on the beach turns out to be someone you don't want to know about. He's someone who has the Americans worried." He held up his hand. "No, don't ask me, I don't know any more than that. But of all the people to get yourself connected to . . ."

"He was dead, Edward. I don't believe either of us planned our meeting."

"Don't be angry. I'm just warning you that this is the worst thing that could have happened. Forget him, he's dead. Think about yourself."

He leaned back in his chair and gave her a quizzical look. "Are you certain there wasn't someone else with you?"

"No," Eva said, "I was alone."

"Well, that's why they're after you. They think you know enough to implicate certain people."

"Then they are themselves guilty."

He shrugged. "Who cares? You're the one in the precarious position. If word gets out that he was murdered, they will try to pin it on you."

"Oh, come, Edward. That's ridiculous."

"So is everything else that's going on around here."

The door to the outer office opened, and he turned off the lamp. "Don't say a word," he whispered and slipped into the other room. The key turned in the lock, and Edward said that he was just leaving. A deeper voice answered.

His wallet was still sitting on the desk. Eva opened it and counted the money. A surprisingly large amount of cash. Edward was clearly moving in larger circles now. No one carried that much money unless he'd just been paid for something he shouldn't have done. She fingered the bills.

He still had the habit of arranging his money from large bills to small. She selected one bill only, tucked it in the pocket of her skirt, and pushed the wallet back over to Edward's side of the desk.

She listened to the voices on the other side of the door. There seemed to be three men, speaking in low cautious voices.

The front door opened and closed. There was silence in the other room. Edward was waiting to see if the men came back. Several minutes later, he unlocked the inside door and sat down, exhausted. "The only advice I have for you is to stay out of it. And that Scottish friend of yours, that one you haven't ever mentioned to me? He should watch his step."

"What friend?"

"Eva. It's been noticed, that's all I'm saying."

An island shrinks down to the size of a boardinghouse, Eva thought, and there are no secrets left. She saw no reason to tell him that McClelland was already gone.

Edward jumped to his feet with a new worry. "You need to get out of here before someone else decides to visit." He ushered her into the hallway.

She turned to say something. He held up his hand. "I don't want to hear another word about it." He slammed the door and locked it from the inside.

She felt like one of the Samoan crabs sold in the street, crabs that clawed their way up the side of a tin bucket only to slide back down again. She was in it without knowing what it was.

She understood Edward's reasoning. She was on the losing side, and he wanted nothing to do with losers.

*W*hen she came home, the Widow was standing in Lehua's yard, her new machete glinting in the moonlight. "If they come to my home, I am ready," she said, lifting the machete. "Go inside," she said quickly. "Talk to Lehua."

"What?"

"Hele mai, hele mai," the Widow said, impatiently waving her towards the door.

Eva hurried into the house.

Lehua was standing in the living room. "Someone has been through the house," she said. "Thank God Jonathan wasn't here."

"We've been robbed?"

"Searched, at least, though nothing seems to be missing. The Widow saw a man leaving through the side door. She thinks he was haole."

Her throat tightened. "Why would someone do that?"

Lehua shrugged. "You should check your room."

She ran up to her bedroom, dropped down on her knees, and ran her hand under the windowsill. The jade was still wedged into the hole she'd carved into the wood.

Everything was in place. Her comb and brush on the vanity. The blanket folded over the end of the bed.

She opened a desk drawer, and knew immediately that someone had been through her papers. Everything had been put back a little too neatly. She checked the wardrobe, the dresser drawers. It was as Lehua had said. Nothing was missing. She fingered Eva Hanson's identification card. Whoever did this has done it before, she thought. Someone who is good at it. Someone who didn't find what he wanted.

*The Floating City · 139*

$\mathcal{B}$y the time she came downstairs, Lehua had shoved wooden wedges under the doors and poured two glasses of rum. Eva took a sip and felt the dry burn run down her throat.

She started to pour the rest of her drink back into the bottle. Most of it spilled over her hand and down the side of the bottle, pooling on the surface of the table. Lehua gave her a look but didn't say anything, just sipped from her own glass, listened to the light rain fingering the roof.

"Are they searching because of Jonathan?"

"I don't know. Maybe just a robbery. My money is in the bank. And yours," Lehua said, pointing at Eva's skirt, "yours is almost gone. Do you think it was that man Rhodes?"

Eva shook her head. "Rhodes would have left muddy foot-prints everywhere. This was someone far more careful."

When the rain stopped, the sound of the swollen river poured into the room, and the wind picked up. Lehua pulled her blouse off her shoulders, lifted her hair off the back of her neck.

From somewhere, a sheet of loose tin shrieked against the side of a house. There was yelling close by, followed by the noise of someone running, and Eva ran her fingers along the edge of the table, feeling as though the sounds were coming out of her-self, the panicked breathing, the slap of bare feet on the wet road.

That friend you haven't mentioned, Edward had said. How would Edward know of McClelland?

She waited until Lehua had gone to bed before taking out the dead woman's identification card and paper. She practiced writing Eva Hanson's signature until her hand ached. She filled five sheets of paper before she was satisfied, and then held each piece of paper over the flame of a candle, the paper flashing as it burned. She opened the window and let the wind take the ash, then blew out the candle and went upstairs in the dark.

The walls of her bedroom were painted white, and the floor covered with worn lauhala matting. An entirely anonymous room. A room she imagined even Eva Hanson might have liked. A person who saw this room wouldn't guess a single thing about her. No one would be able to tell what she did for a living. No one would see that she was obsessed over a dead man and falling in love with another, a man she knew nothing about, who had left her with the breath of a stranger trapped in a glass ball.

*B*y early January 1895, just two years after Queen Liliʻuokalaniʻs forced abdication, the Royalists had taken matters into their own hands. The evening announced itself with a full moon that rose quickly out of the sea. Moonlight poured down on a Royalist boat, turning it as visible as a black cutout on white paper. It was bright enough to count each man on deck.

The boat came ashore at Diamond Head.

Men waded through the waves carrying heavy boxes over their heads, piling them on the sand up above the high tide line. The piles of boxes grew, and the men stood in nervous circles. A quick decision was made to hide the guns in the nearby wilderness of spindly kiawe trees.

Deep holes were quickly dug in the sand, and a layer of leaves was spread at the bottom of each hole, and the boxes were lowered as carefully as coffins, then covered with more leaves and sand. The backs of the shovels were pulled across the sand to flatten it, and then a branch was used to sweep away their tracks.

Halfway back to town the wind started and the tops of the trees tangled, and a light rain splattered down on the Royalists as they headed into Honolulu.

# Fifteen

In the early days of January 1895, the women now traveled silent as shadows, spreading what news there was like a contagious disease, while their husbands broke off ties to hidden mistresses, took their money out of the bank, quietly armed themselves.

The men in the streets didn't know what to do next, so they ran, their legs stretching down Beretania Street, passing Iolani Palace and then over to the statue of King Kamehameha, who glared down at them. The men chased after anything, even after those who were simply running away.

The lepers were the most terrified of all.

People threw their money away in sailors' bars, or on cock-fights, or even the lottery. The Americans bought as much land as they could, with a greed checked only by geography. There were more daredevils, more tempting of fate, more proposals of marriage between people who wouldn't have glanced at each other a month ago.

At home, Lehua cooked an extra chicken, took the silver framed daguerreotype of her mother and her koa wood bowls and hid them up in the crawl space above the ceiling, bought enough opium to last out the month.

The tourist boats still kept coming, and Lehua's Hawaiian language class was full. Her newest substitute for good morning was: I am a fool. When the tourists announced this, the shopkeepers smiled and nodded in agreement.

The Widow found two centipedes in her bed and was convinced that the Americans had put them there. Her nephew was missing, and she blamed the Americans for that as well.

All the people wanted their future told, and those who had once laughed at the very idea of fortunetelling were now Eva's steadiest customers. What did they want to hear? Your life will be full, and interesting. Your children will always love you.

What she actually said was this: Look both ways. Be careful of sudden friendships and the knock on the door.

They came to ask about Queen Lili'uokalani. Eva was a fluent liar, yet she wouldn't lie about the Queen. She couldn't say that the monarchy would be restored. She didn't see it. Nor could she say that the Queen would be safe. So she refused to say anything at all about Lili'uokalani, and her clients became impatient with her honesty and turned to the other fortunetellers in town, those who would tell them what they wanted to hear. For the first time in her life she was telling the truth, and it was as she'd always suspected. The truth was costing her money.

Even Tomas was changing. Before, he'd spent most of his days sleeping in his hammock, with Lucky perched on his chest. Today, she found him in the front yard, hurling knives into a bright red target attached to a coconut tree. He looked at Eva and smiled, and the thought came to her that if she'd been born fifty years ago she would have fallen in love with him.

She sat down on the steps of the lanai and watched Tomas pull a knife out of each of his boots. His old hands shook, but his aim was still deadly accurate.

She didn't need to ask who the target was.

He yanked the knives out of the target and turned to her. "Eva, you know what I keep thinking about?"

Eva looked at the knives and declined to answer.

"Petroglyphs. You know what they are, carvings in the rock, like signatures. They're all around us. Here on Oahu but on the Big Island as well. Torsos, spears. The ones that intrigue me, though, are the games. The early Hawaiians carved games into the rocks, games people played to pass the time. A kind of checkers. Maybe chess, who knows?"

He flung a knife, and Eva shifted her weight on the stairs.

"I used to wonder, what were they waiting for? Safety? The weather to change? Maybe the volcano was erupting? Now I know what it was. They were waiting for the enemy to make the first move."

"Perhaps they were just playing checkers," Eva said, attempting to calm him down.

"No, they were preparing themselves." Tomas threw a knife and looked over towards the street. Eva followed his glance. A man on a bicycle emerged between the green shadows of the trees.

Without thinking, she pulled back into the shadowy lanai.

Tomas squinted at the figure. "No, it's not one of them," he said, meaning soldiers.

McClelland pedaled into the sunlight. His basket was overflowing with flowers, and he passed by without seeing them.

"That man moves like a sailor," Tomas said approvingly. He distrusted people who'd never had to balance themselves against the movement of waves. People who still believed the earth was solid.

Tomas turned to her and frowned when he saw her expression. "Ah, Eva. I don't claim to know what you're going through, but I can tell you this. You're too young to let pride drown your poor heart. Believe me, regret is a terrible companion in old age."

He walked over to the lanai and gave her shoulder a gentle push. "Go," he said. "At least hear what he has to say."

"How do you know about him?"

"You think you're the only one around here with second sight? Actually, the milkman told me. Go on, then."

Eva felt like a house on fire. What was there to save, what was there to leave behind? And when people saved themselves, what exactly did they save themselves for?

She ducked through the hedge and met McClelland pushing the bicycle through the long grass. He stopped when he saw her, and the air turned liquid for a moment. What will happen next? she wondered, panicked. Will he disappear again? She knew what Tomas would say. So what if he does.

He smiled. "I came to have my fortune read," he said. He scooped up the flowers and let the bicycle fall onto the grass.

She knew exactly which streets he'd taken by the flowers he'd stolen. Orchids from the Widow's rivals, and the pikake that washed over the fences and spread a scented wave out into the street.

He held out the flowers, and she realized what scared her most were normal events, the knock on the door, the package left on the step. The heart let loose.

She made no move to take the flowers, and they slipped from his arms, a trail of petals that followed their path across the lawn and up the wooden stairs of the lanai. Eva stopped to slip out of her shoes, and he did the same.

"So, here we are," he said, following her into the parlor.

Here I am, she thought. I have no idea where you are. His presence was as wounding as his absence.

They looked at each other. There were chickens rustling under the house, a strange whooshing sound like salt water trapped in an ear. Eva felt unsettled by it.

His eyes traveled over Lehua's tapa and koa wood bowls, the

old harpoon, a cluster of bamboo fishing poles, a spyglass, whale bones.

McClelland touched a fishing pole, then reached forward and nearly touched Eva's hair. She took a step backwards and his hand dropped.

Behind her, Eva heard Lehua's bare feet walking across the worn lauhala mat. She was carrying a tray with glasses and a pitcher of tea.

Eva watched Lehua and McClelland take each other's measure, while feigning lack of interest. Both would be complete failures in her business.

"I'm here for my fortune," McClelland told her.

"Of course you are," Lehua answered.

No one moved to pour the tea.

McClelland waited for Eva to pick up his hand and offer a future, but she was so tired of it, taking the hand of anyone and pretending she could see the whole world in it. Glimpses, side views, winks, that was all anyone could hope for. Illumination was for saints.

And betrayal, she thought, is for the rest of us.

"Perhaps this isn't a good time for a visit?" he asked nervously.

Lehua quickly glanced at Eva. "No, no, it's fine," she said, reaching for the pitcher of tea. Lehua poured three glasses, and disappeared.

McClelland ran his hands nervously through his hair, then tapped the edge of his glass.

Again, Eva wondered if he had a wife. So many did. Wives and mistresses tucked away all over the world, and if they were lucky, they'd never learn of each other's existences.

He picked up the glass and set it down again. "I've been out of town," he ventured. "I went to see someone. A friend."

She felt something akin to seasickness. It comes now, she

thought, sitting down. He will tell me that he is in love with someone. Or worse, married.

He pulled a chair forward and sat down facing her.

She refused to look at him. She stared at his legs instead, his knees close enough to knock with her fist. What was that game? Your fist was an egg and you broke it across someone's knee and the egg ran down his legs.

I can't bear this, she thought, putting her hand on the edge of the chair to steady herself.

"It's my brother," he said.

She was suddenly, selfishly elated. It wasn't another woman, it was something else entirely.

"My brother is younger than I am." He took her hand and turned it over. "Pretend," he said, "that this is the palm of a young man. He has followed his older brother to Hawaii, all the way from Edinburgh." He paused.

Edinburgh, she thought, breaking the word apart. The chickens were quiet under the house, and the clock from the next room sounded the hour. She waited.

Finally, McClelland continued. "He traveled to Hawaii because the older brother had written home about how beautiful it is here, how the two of them could go into business. The older brother exaggerated, of course, because he missed his family. He had no right to say any of this, because the younger brother was almost too young to leave home." He shrugged. "And yet people don't move to the other side of the world because their life is good."

He abruptly stood up.

"Sit down," she said softly, and he did.

"You know this as well as anyone, Eva, the desire to travel is either in a person or it isn't. Some people are born with a restlessness that can't be put down. So the younger brother made the long trip, and he too loved this island, and the brothers worked hard. For a few years everything was fine; they weren't rich, but they were happy to be where they were and doing better than expected.

"The brother loved the sea, he loved to swim, to fish. He climbed coconut trees, cut down the nuts with a machete. He's always been very athletic. When he was a boy he could run backwards faster than most could run forwards."

He took hold of Eva's hand. "Then the younger brother got a spot on his leg. He ignored it, like a good Scotsman. After all, what's a spot on your leg? Then another one appeared, and another. He didn't want to worry his older brother, who was so busy working he couldn't see what was right in front of him.

"And then the spots became worse, turning into sores, and his foot began to give him such pain that he limped. And still the older brother didn't see it, he was busy because they were starting to lose money, there was more tax on imported goods. The younger brother worried that the business was failing because of himself, that it was somehow his fault. That's how young he was."

He looked down, surprised to be holding her hand.

"And by the time the older brother did finally see it, it was in his face. There is no boat on earth that will take a boy all the way back to Scotland when he has visible leprosy. It would kill our mother to see him."

He turned to the window. "They think perhaps he caught it from getting a tattoo down in Chinatown. That he was infected from a needle. Who knows?"

Eva thought of Lehua's mother. "He is hiding," she said.

He nodded. "I've moved him to a safer place. I don't want him sent to Molokai."

"It isn't your fault," Eva said softly.

"Ah, yes. It's entirely my fault. He was a boy, and I offered him an adventure. The worst of it is that he doesn't blame me."

Eva touched his shoulder, felt it shaking under her hand. "He loves you."

McClelland nodded, staring at the floor.

"Who takes care of him?"

"There are people who watch over him. I do . . . favors for them."

"Favors?"

He waved his hand nervously. "Imports, mostly."

Eva understood, finally. Guns. So he is on the side of the Royalists, she thought. Well, who wouldn't be? Edward, for one, unless the tide turned.

His eyes flicked towards the window and back, fast as bird's wings. He was seeing nothing.

Eva remembered the paintings covering the walls of his house, the young man with the same eyes as McClelland. "He is the painter?"

"Yes. He does self-portraits and paints the woman who takes care of him. Actually, they take care of each other. He paints anything that crosses his path. Flowers," he said, motioning to the jar Lehua filled with his flowers. "He loves color. And it keeps him from being too lonely . . ." he trailed off.

She glanced up at him, wondering if it was the sadness of other people that made you fall in love with them, the weight they carried that first turned you in their direction.

He picked up his tea and gave an awkward laugh. "I think I just did your job for you, told my own fortune."

"Most people do."

His hand shook as he set down the tea, and she took both his hands and held them until he was calm, and they sat that way without speaking, for such a long time that the light was doing something odd in the room, leapfrogging from place to place.

Her grandmother had always told her to keep track of her heart. Where's that heart of yours right now? Mormor would whisper sometimes when they were sitting at the back of a rented hall, listening to her mother's raving attempts to catch the spiritual world and pull it into her purse.

Right here, Eva would whisper back, tapping the thin cage of her chest. The heart wasn't something to let loose.

"I am being watched," she said. "By a man named Rhodes and I don't know who else."

He nodded. "The government has their eye on many people in this town. Thank God they're not very good at it."

He leaned forward and kissed her.

She kissed him back. It was sailing blindfolded, like those sailors who believed that the world ended in a cliff and that their boats would fall right off the face of the earth.

What if they fell into the arms of a woman? Was that the same thing?

She led him upstairs, glancing at the door to the storeroom, feeling Jonathan's absence.

In her room, Eva pulled his shirt loose and slipped it back off his shoulders and let it fall to the floor. He closed his eyes, and she placed her fingers between the bones of his ribs.

He lifted the edge of her camisole, and she raised her arms and felt the brush of silk over her face.

Outside, a bird was crying, and the wind picked up and rattled the windows. Somewhere in the house, an open door slammed shut. A flash of lightning illuminated them, turning their skin a pale bluish white. Against the wall his shadow hovered above her, and as she pulled him down his shadow disappeared, and she tasted the salt in the small hollow above his collarbone.

Who is ever ready when her own good luck arrives?

*J*ust two nights after the Royalists had hurriedly buried the guns in the sand at Waikiki Beach, they went back to retrieve them.

The men were as nervous as if this was the actual night of the attack, with the sense they were not simply digging boxes of guns out of the damp sand but already stepping into the future, loaded guns in hand, taking back their country.

The wooden boxes were loaded into carts, and kindling was piled over the top to hide the boxes. Once more, they set off for Honolulu.

The following morning, volunteers arrived at the two places designated by the Royalist leaders. The wooden boxes were pried opened and guns handed out. The crowd grew as new Royalists declared themselves, and by afternoon there were twice as many men.

The mood was oddly festive. One man wore a coconut hat woven into the shape of a derby. Another brought his ukulele as well as his hunting knife, which he used to slice a large Republic flag into pieces. He tied a strip of flag around his arm. It felt good, like a first step.

Some of the men spoke in words that polished the future into something almost too bright to be believed, while others threw shadows across the day. There were those who truly wanted the monarchy to be reinstated, and others who were Royalists simply because it suited their economic needs.

# Sixteen

McClelland left just before dawn. Eva locked the door behind him, then stood still in the dark, listening. There was the whirr of McClelland's bicycle tires in the wet grass. There was the sound of guava juice dripping into the pans in the kitchen, in preparation for guava jelly. Still, she sensed someone else's presence. She went upstairs and tried the storeroom door. It was unlocked, with enough light coming through the window to see that it was empty.

She came back downstairs the way Malia did, hugging the wall to make less noise. The living room was empty. At the window, a curtain lifted and fell in the breeze.

She found him in the kitchen, standing amid the dripping muslin sacks holding the guava pulp. Jonathan wasn't surprised to see her. Eva doubted that anything surprised him.

Jonathan gestured at the sacks. "They look like cow's bladders," he said, and Eva laughed without meaning to.

"Why are you here?" she asked.

He didn't answer her question. He put his hand at the top of one of the muslin sacks, then quickly drew his finger down the length of the fabric, and the liquid seeped through along the path of his finger.

"You've made jelly before?" Eva asked.

He shrugged. "I've seen it done, though not quite like this. Where is Lehua?"

"Sleeping."

"She doesn't need to know that I am here."

$\mathcal{T}$hat morning, she boiled the guava juice into jelly and poured it into clean jars, sealing each with a layer of paraffin. She lined the jars along the windowsill, and the sun lit them like stained glass.

Jonathan's reappearance worried her. Something would happen soon, before the month was out, and she needed to distance herself from it. It was time to sell the jade.

She glanced out the window. At the orphanage, the young girls stepped into burlap sacks, pulled them up to their waists, hopped wildly to the fence, and slapped it three times with the palms of their hands. They then turned and hopped back towards the lanai of the orphanage.

Their strange game quickly disintegrated into a war. They slapped and pushed each other, with the one crying the loudest the one most often pushed down into the mud.

Eva wondered if she'd ever played games like that, with a rage that could only take you as far as a fence and back. Escape, she silently urged them. Throw down the burlap sacks and run into Honolulu.

She turned away from the window to ask Lehua to explain the game, but Lehua had smoked too much opium and was now lying on the punee and could not be roused.

Eva crouched down next to her and touched her face. "Come, I'll wash your hair."

Lehua shook her head and turned to the wall. Eva rubbed her

back and Lehua shifted, pulled up like a cat. Eva covered her with a light blanket and went back to the window.

The girls' limbs moved erratically under the burlap, like a sack of kittens on their way to being drowned. If children are the measure of a place, Eva thought, then this island has truly gone mad.

Odd behavior now ruled all of Honolulu. Several days ago, a boy on a pier had caught a fish so large that it pulled him into the water, dragging him out into the middle of the bay. That was the last anyone had seen of him. He could have just let go.

She mentioned that she was going to the jewelry shop on Beretania Street, but Lehua was beyond hearing, beyond caring, stretched out on the punee, eyes closed and fingers laced, the way the bodies of the dead are arranged.

"Lehua," she whispered, "I'm leaving now." Lehua's eyelids fluttered. Eva gently unlaced her fingers and slipped out of the house.

*A* small bell rang as Eva pushed open the door of the jewelry shop. The jeweler was busy with a missionary woman who leaned forward over the counter. She was pale, whittled down the way most of them were, in direct opposition to the Hawaiian women, who were voluptuous, carrying their weight like a gift.

She was showing the jeweler the braided hair of her dead sister, asking what the long rope of hair could be made into.

"A beautiful necklace," the jeweler suggested. "Long, with intricate braidwork. It will be as elegant as a strand of opera pearls."

"Oh, is there enough hair for that?" the woman asked excitedly.

Eva moved to the other end of the shop, as far away as she could get.

She remembered her own childhood braid, and a day when

her mother poured basin water over her hair, then washed it with the softest soap, rinsed it with water scented with chamomile, and threaded a thin ribbon through her braid.

They went through Oslo to a shop where there was a discussion of money. Eva wasn't paying attention. Her mother was always haggling over money, and the price of a bit of meat, or a pair of used shoes. Suddenly, without a warning, her mother lifted the braid and a shop assistant cut it off, leaving Eva as shocked as she'd ever been, as if they'd taken off an arm or a leg.

The woman turned to Eva. "It's my sister's hair," she said. "May I ask your opinion?"

Eva stared down at the long length of hair. What would be bearable? "A small brooch," Eva told her, "a very small brooch." She held her fingers up, no more than half an inch apart.

The jeweler frowned at her, and the woman turned away. A necklace it was.

After the woman left the shop, the jeweler shook his finger at Eva. "You could lose me business," he scolded. "The longer pieces take more time and pay a great deal more than a brooch. And she brought in a horsetail's worth of hair. They outlaw leis, and yet they do this. There's no understanding these people, eh?" They both laughed. The laugh of those in the same business.

Eva showed him the jade, and again he suggested that they try to sell it in San Francisco. "As I've said, a piece of jewelry this expensive will be recognized. Before, you were hesitating to let this go. Now you seem in a hurry."

If he knew she was anxious, she wouldn't make half the money. "No, I'd just rather have the cash."

He nodded, clearly not believing her.

"There was something else I was hoping you could help me with. If I needed to find out the identity of someone, and I didn't want to involve the police, who would I go to?"

He glanced up at her carefully, as if deciding the value of a piece of jewelry. He noticed a smudge on the glass case and wiped it with his cuff. "There is no reason to put yourself in harm's way," he finally said. "This is no time to be asking questions."

"Why not?"

"You remember last fall, not long after you came to Hawaii, there were Royalists caught bringing in guns."

Eva nodded, remembering.

"So, yesterday, I hear the same kind of rumors that I heard last fall."

Jonathan, Eva thought. That explained his presence.

"I think it is better that you are not seen coming here again. I will contact you when a buyer is found."

She knew what he meant. He didn't want a trail of bad fortune leading to him.

Eva waited.

He finally looked up at her and shook his head. "Well, stubborn Eva, then go see Kaina."

"Kaina?"

"You know who he is, the bartender at the American Club."

"He works for the Americans?" she asked.

He pulled a key from his pocket and locked a drawer. "He works for them, yes. Who doesn't, these days? But he is still one of us," he added, his eyes sliding away from her like boats.

*E*very political group has its Judas, the snake hidden in the grass, the cup of poisoned wine. For the Royalists, he surfaced just hours before their planned attack on the Republic.

The traitor went over to the other side and warned the Republic of the impending battle.

The response was swift. Republic politicians and soldiers gathered, both outraged and excited that their new government now needed to be protected. They counted their new guns and passed out ammunition. Men piled into wagons, and others rode horses, and together they surrounded the home of the leader of the Royalists. At a signal, they opened fire.

Within the house, there was a sudden confusion, everyone yelling at once, scrambling to the windows to fire back.

Far outnumbered, the Royalists soon scattered up into the dry brush of Diamond Head, a rough unsettled area with a steep slope that led up towards an open caldera. The Hawaiians knew the terrain and were faster on their feet, but the Republic soldiers had cannons and fired across the entire side of the mountain, leaving small craters gouged into the rock.

The Republic sharpshooters did their work, firing at those Royalists who were not fast enough, even firing at those who had turned around and stripped off their shirts to wave surrender. Those who weren't shot fanned out across the slopes, climbing from one valley to the next.

There were twenty government soldiers for every Royalist, all of them with new guns and boots and canteens of water attached to new belts. Some of the Royalists were barefoot, and all of them were hungry.

# Seventeen

*E*very shade of green that existed was right in front of them. The yellow-green of bamboo, the falling down green of an old hut, the young green of banana leaves, the dark grass where the mongoose hid, the chartreuse of the kukui tree, McClelland's green eyes, the pinkish green of a ripening mango, the translucent green limu from the sea, the bright green light that flashed before sunrise.

There was a green ohia tree on the trail in front of them, a green so old Eva thought it had to be the very first color on earth. She thought of the first woman who might have seen that tree, a Polynesian woman who'd come to Hawaii from somewhere inside the triangle of Tonga, Samoa, and the Marquesas. A woman who passed this very place and stopped to pick a leaf of ohia and rub it into green dust between her fingers.

Eva and McClelland moved quietly, not speaking. Because of yesterday's fighting between the Royalists and the government soldiers, a man hiking up into the mountains looked suspicious, but a man and a woman could pretend to be on a picnic, pretend that they didn't know anything about the war, that they hadn't noticed the crowds of soldiers filling the streets of Honolulu.

Yesterday, Eva had left the jeweler's shop, turned a corner. The next street over was full of government soldiers, patrolling the streets and knocking on doors.

A man told her there had been fighting between the soldiers and the Royalists.

"Where are the Royalists now?" Eva asked.

"Up towards Diamond Head. The government sent up their sharpshooters, eh? So they can pick them off like goats," he yelled.

A wagon of soldiers passed and a shot was fired somewhere, and Eva turned and ran back to the jeweler's. His door was locked, a closed sign still swinging from a hook.

She stayed on the back streets, hiding when any soldiers approached. It had taken her an hour to get home.

And now, today, she was taking the risk of hiking up into the mountains to deliver food to McClelland's brother Ethan. It was a good time, Eva thought, to question one's sanity. With the curfew and roadblocks springing up, McClelland worried that he would no longer be able to bring his brother the supplies he needed.

Along the way, McClelland scolded himself, saying he should have known it would happen by now. He should have already taken supplies to his brother.

So he knew about the attack, Eva thought.

They hiked through the dusty afternoon, surrounded by the green smell of trampled grass and the sweet scent of ginger, heady enough to turn a bee into a fool.

There were children playing in a stream that ran alongside the path, children the colors of honey and polished coconut and freshly turned earth. It took Eva a moment to figure out what made them so different from the girls in the orphanage. They were happy.

The heat moved over their bodies like a wet hand, and McClelland's eyes were filled with a green heat, and Eva picked a wildflower and threaded it into his buttonhole, wondering if it were ever possible to separate a person from the place you met him.

Their mood was abruptly broken by a group of soldiers standing in a circle around an old woman who clearly didn't understand why she'd been stopped or what they were asking her.

"It begins," McClelland said, under his breath. He greeted the soldiers, but they only glanced at him before turning back to the woman.

She looked at Eva helplessly.

Eva spoke to the soldiers. "She's an old woman. She obviously doesn't speak English."

It was the wrong thing to say. The soldiers gave Eva their full attention.

"Can't you just let her go?" Eva asked. "She's not doing anything wrong."

A soldier shrugged impatiently. "And what are the two of you doing up here?"

"A picnic," Eva said, linking her arm into McClelland's.

"Don't you know what's going on in Honolulu?"

"Is something happening?" Eva asked. The soldier rolled his eyes and turned back to the woman.

McClelland pulled out a package of cigarettes, and offered them to the soldiers. "Good for the mosquitoes," he said.

"What?"

"The smoke. It keeps the mosquitoes down." One soldier set down his gun and lit a cigarette, then slid the pack into his own pocket.

Eva motioned the woman away, and she slowly backed off. A moment later, she turned and ran, the leathered soles of her feet visible.

The soldiers laughed.

McClelland was told to take everything out of his rucksack and place it on the ground.

*The Floating City · 167*

Sketchbook and paints. Food.

A soldier opened a jar of paint and sniffed. He made a face and turned to show the paint to the others, and they talked among themselves for a moment. McClelland was still smiling, but Eva felt a wet trickle of tension running down her back.

The bandages were harder to explain.

"Women's affairs," Eva said, and the youngest soldier blushed. They were quickly told to pack up and continue with their hike.

"Women's affairs," McClelland repeated, once they were out of hearing. "That was good."

The road became steeper, veering upward to the razored peaks. Everywhere she looked, Eva saw the end of something. Abandoned huts with no roofs, taro patches gone to ruin, weed-filled pastureland with a white pipi bird perched on the bony fence of a cow's back. A papaya farm grown wild. They came to a ditch and jumped over the bones of a water buffalo that were splayed open like the hull of a boat.

On Oahu, there was smallpox, venereal disease, and whatever else the boats had brought in from the rest of the world. Less than a century ago, there had been 250,000 Hawaiians, and now there were fewer than 40,000.

It was like traveling through a graveyard, and it was hard to imagine any future at all when there was so little left in the present.

They hiked under wet branches that filtered the light like colored glass, and in a search for sun the green ti grew tall and spindly. Low rock walls cut across the forest and disappeared. It was believed that the walls were made by the menehunes, the little people who lived in the mountains and worked only at night, building walls and fishponds and creating mischief. The menehunes were shy and hid from people. Who could blame them?

Eva was still nervous, expecting more soldiers, but McClelland reassured her that they were too lazy to hike this far unless they were chasing someone.

Soon after, they entered a small clearing holding a hut and a rain barrel. McClelland whistled two high notes followed by a lower one.

A boy about seventeen years old stepped out onto the small lanai. He wore a long sleeved palaka shirt, long pants, and the same smile as McClelland. He nodded shyly in Eva's direction and ran to McClelland.

So young, Eva thought, her throat constricting. The disease was visible in his hands and along one side of his jawline, and he kept that side of his face turned away.

Eva moved quickly to him, picking up his hand to introduce herself.

An old woman appeared out of the shade and spoke to Mc-Clelland in a low voice, and he bent over to hug her, telling her about the soldiers and the roadblock.

He turned and introduced her to Eva.

Ethan's hut was just one room, divided by a rough curtain. Paintings and drawings were tacked onto the walls. Many of them were of the old woman, whose name was Nahi. In some paintings she was smiling, with trees behind her. Others were of McClelland, and several were self-portraits. Eva looked closely at those, and it was clear that Ethan was documenting his illness, painting it as it showed in his face.

Nahi served them rainwater sweetened with lemon and sugar in the same etched glasses that McClelland owned.

"All the way from Scotland," said McClelland, holding one up. The light hovered around the glass like a bee.

Ethan smiled and shook his head, said something in Hawaiian to Nahi, who laughed. He told Eva that she couldn't trust anything that his brother said. He called him Loftus, a nickname from their childhood.

"Has he given you his real name?" Ethan asked.

"No," Eva said, "but then I haven't told him mine, either."

McClelland opened the rucksack and set each item on the

wooden steps. A bottle of milk. A new shirt. Dried beans. A game of Hawaiian checkers. Ethan was pleased by each offering, but especially so by the bottle of ink and the Japanese brushes. He leapt up and said he must paint all three of them immediately, and the old woman laughed and said no, not another painting, but Ethan had already gone into the hut for paper.

He attached a leather and wood contraption to his hand, allowing him to hold a brush. They sat next to Nahi for several ink drawings, which Ethan did quickly, his strokes fast and sure. He didn't show them the drawings. He said they must come back another time for a more finished painting.

In the late afternoon, when McClelland picked up his rucksack, Ethan couldn't hide his disappointment.

"You're not staying any longer?" he asked.

"We have to leave before it's too dark to hike back down the mountain."

"But that will be hours from now."

"They're looking for Royalists, Ethan. And it's a long walk," he added gently. "I don't want to tire you."

"No, I'm fine. Really."

McClelland pulled his brother to him, his hands moving unconsciously across Ethan's face.

Nahi came to the doorway and waved to them, then took Ethan's arm and led him indoors.

On the way down the mountain, Eva worried about running into the same soldiers and having to explain the empty rucksack. Along the way she picked guavas to fill the bag, but when they came to the road, the soldiers were gone.

They didn't speak about Ethan. It was easier not to speak about what couldn't be changed.

It was dark by the time they arrived at McClelland's house. He heated water for a bath, and Eva slipped out of her clothes and stepped into the tin tub, her feet aching in the hot water.

He poured a pitcher of water over her and the warmth rushed

down her body, a small waterfall between her breasts, her belly. He poured water between her fingers, over her blistered hands, then bundled her into towels that scraped against her skin.

He unrolled a Japanese quilt with a pattern of poppies and birds and shook it into the air.

They slipped under the quilt and Eva quickly pulled him on top of her, needing to feel the weight of the living, as if that could keep everything around her from disappearing.

*A* life changes in an instant, this is what the past teaches.

A horse-drawn carriage clattered up the driveway of Queen Liliʻuokalaniʻs private home and stopped next to the lanai. Government soldiers stepped out of the carriage and came briskly up the stairs. The doorbell rang in quick jabs.

When the maid opened the door, there was no greeting from the soldiers. Liliʻuokalani stood in the hallway, waiting.

The thinnest soldier walked into the house without invitation, moving around the maid as if she were simply a piece of furniture. He held up a document, moist from his sticky hands, and began to read. He was young and nervous, and stood too close to the Queen, his sweat dripping down onto the edge of her black skirt, steady as a metronome.

Noticing this, he flushed and took a step back, then continued reading.

When he came to the part where it was written that Liliʻuokalani had committed an act of treason against the Republic of Hawaii, his voice wavered, and the words were gone in a wash of ink and perspiration. He was already reading from memory, already seeing himself as part of a historical act.

The soldier informed her that she was to be taken to Iolani Palace. The carriage ride lasted only several minutes, but it seemed a lifetime. The soldier seated across from her wore a gun strapped across his chest and an expression to let her know he was ready to use it.

Lili'uokalani had not been allowed in Iolani Palace since she was forced to abdicate two years earlier, and it was a shock to see it in such disrepair. The rooms were stripped of all belongings, even the gold mirrors set into the koa wood walls had been stolen, the walls knife-gouged where the mirrors had been pried loose. The tall feather kahilis had disappeared. Only the glass doors etched with the ghosts of women were still intact.

The soldiers offered Lili'uokalani a chair, but she refused to sit down.

In the throne room, an official of the Republic of Hawaii charged her with treason. The soldiers took her up the wide stairs to a small room at the front of the palace. They told the Queen this was where she would be held.

After the door closed and locked behind her, she removed her hat and her long black veil. She ran her finger along the dusty windowsill and then took her diamond ring and with an unsteady hand she scratched the date into the glass. January 16, 1895.

# Eighteen

The next morning, McClelland made coffee while Eva un-packed guavas from the satchel, covering the kitchen table with fruit, more than they could possibly eat. She laughed and promised to make jelly.

A neighbor came to the door and McClelland invited him in. He shook his head, insisting that McClelland come outside. They stepped over to the plumeria tree, and Eva watched them talking quietly. The man was becoming angry, gesturing violently with his hands. McClelland patted his shoulder and turned back to the house.

Eva quickly sat down.

McClelland came through the door, shaking his head. "You won't believe this, Eva. My neighbor tells me that the Republic's soldiers have just taken Queen Lili'uokalani prisoner."

While most rumors could be dismissed, there were others as clear as a blade in the small of the back. As much as Eva didn't want to believe it, she knew it was true. She leaned against the table, suddenly sick to her stomach.

"Are you all right?"

She stood up. She quickly found her jacket and went to the door.

"Wait, Eva."

She shook her head. "I have to find out for myself."

"Just a minute, I'll go with you."

"No," Eva said, thinking of Ethan. "It's better that you don't."

She left the house, joining a stampede of bare feet running towards the palace, the town rocking side to side with the rumor. She ran past a woman waving a sandalwood fan, her feet soaking in a bucket of water, and an old man with a machete who stared up into a breadfruit tree. She passed the closed down newspaper offices, and the eyes of politicians in photographers' windows.

A crowd surrounded the Queen's private home. Eva pushed towards the front, watching the soldiers swarm over the Queen's home like an invasion of soft crabs, spilling belongings across the front lawn and over the driveway, searching for documents.

Eva worked her way to the front of the crowd, edging close to a large pile of papers and books scattered across the lawn. A soldier stared at her quizzically, and she realized that she was standing too near the documents, too far from the street. She backed away slowly, his eyes following her. There was no reason to draw too much attention to herself.

Soldiers hacked through the gardenia bushes, pulled lilikoi vines off the fence, and trampled the flowerbeds that stretched the length of the property. The branches and mounds of dirt grew and sweat stained the backs of the soldiers' shirts. They cut down fruit trees and pulled the large ferns out by the roots. Every potted plant on the lanai was turned over, leaving behind a mess of broken pottery and soil.

People stood in groups, dread thickening the air. A woman at the front of the crowd was sobbing, and Eva put her arm around her, but the woman saw that Eva was haole and shrugged off her arm.

A young soldier digging up the lawn hit against something hard with his shovel. He let out a small cry of satisfaction, and a mob gathered around him.

A wooden box was lifted up out of the hole, and the dirt was carefully brushed off with a whisk broom.

The captain was called out of Lili'uokalani's house. A soldier went off to find a crowbar, and while he waited, the captain paced back and forth in front of the box. The crowd was silent, waiting. When the crowbar arrived, the captain held it up for everyone to see. He pried open the box, which held bundles of oiled rags. The captain unwrapped one of the bundles and held up a gun.

Eva had seen it before, Lili'uokalani surrounded by wooden boxes. She thought of the locked storeroom upstairs, Jonathan coming and going during the night.

The mood turned angry. Threats were yelled at the soldiers, who responded with obscene gestures. It would have been bedlam if the Queen hadn't always insisted that her people stay calm and behave like Christians. Yet what was there to do, people grumbled, when the Christians themselves no longer behaved like Christians?

Reporters from foreign newspapers wandered through the crowd asking questions, and then, ignoring what they were told, wrote down their own answers. The real news from Hawaii rarely reached the rest of the world, just bits and pieces of gossip. When journalists came to the islands, they were surprised that the Queen even spoke English. From what had been written about her, they were expecting a woman with a bone in her nose, rather than a devout Christian concerned with the health and education of her people.

In the confusion, the pickpockets were already at work, moving fast as birds over freshly turned soil.

A grenade was found and held up for the crowd to see. The man standing next to Eva pointed out that the Americans could

*The Floating City · 177*

find a torture chamber if they intended it. Why stop at a grenade?

The crowd moved like a sea anemone, expanding and shrinking depending on the news. It had the feel of a nightmare played out in daylight. Just standing there was bad luck. When someone pushed against her, Eva didn't bother to see who it was, she just shoved back.

At the edge of the commotion, a missionary stood on a box, crying out about the wickedness of Queen Lili'uokalani and all those who would dare follow her.

"The Hawaiians must choose God," he yelled in a high voice. "The Kingdom is above us," he said, "not in front of us." His hand shook as he pointed to the boxes of guns. "And the end of the century will be the end of the world."

Eva pushed through the crowd, and when she came close to the missionary she gave his wooden box a solid kick. It was just enough to send him tumbling into the muddy street.

*P*ursued by the Republic soldiers, those Royalists who had not been captured continued across the island, hiking to the very top of the Pali. They stopped just before the sharp descent down the windward side, a cliff so steep that it stole the breath from their mouths.

On the windcarved rocks just below them was a scattering of bones where the battle between Kamehameha the Great and the King of Oahu had taken place. Kamehameha, the great unifier of the islands, had won that decisive battle.

All those brave warriors who were killed and thrown off the side of the steep cliff, only to blow back up in the strong wind that raced up the side of the mountain.

What happened to the living when the dead reappeared a moment later? It was possible to kill a man, but how could you kill his ghost? You had to wait until you were dead yourself.

It has been a short reign from Kamehameha the Great to the present time. From King Kamehameha to Liholiho to Kauikeaouli to Alexander Liholiho to Lot Kamehameha to Lunalilo to Kalakaua now to Queen Lili'uokalani, all of it in under a hundred years, and *the beginnings still visible in the remains of those warriors, their bones broken against the rocks, eroded by the wind. Bones left undisturbed for nearly a hundred years, now bleached white as a missionary collar.*

# Nineteen

$\mathcal{D}$uring low tide, the sea sucked back and the town showed its underbelly of mud and trash. Eva picked her way through last night's shipwrecks of fish heads and empty whiskey bottles, lobster shells and the sharp smell of urine. A smashed straw boater with a bleeding ribbon floated on a puddle of mud.

Yesterday, the Queen had been taken prisoner, but today the business of Honolulu resumed as if nothing out of the ordinary had happened. The trams were working, the saloons were filled with the daily mix of sailors, music, and fighting. The sides of the roads were crowded with scrimshaw, children's toys, Bibles, and opium pipes, all of it displayed on lauhala mats placed over the dirt. Everyone was open for business. Drygoods, churches, lottery offices, prostitutes.

Barefoot children marched behind the soldiers, carrying sharpened sticks and overripe breadfruit that they pretended were rifles and hand grenades, throwing them at the soldiers, and then disappearing back into the crowd. The soldiers were never certain if the squirming child they ran down and held at the back of the neck was actually the guilty one.

Eva turned at the corner by the photographer's studio. In the window, dusty faces in cheap frames stared out at nothing. In Honolulu, only politicians and brides were willing to leave their images on paper. Eva stared in the photographer's window, pretending interest in a faded photograph of haole men in bathing costumes.

Next door to the studio was the American Club, the place the jeweler told Eva to go for information about the dead man. Kaina, the club bartender, was known to be honest, and Eva was beginning to wonder if he might be the only man left in Honolulu who could make that claim.

She pushed open the door and stepped into a large dark room. Nightclubs were dismal places to find yourself during the day, with the smell of the previous night's mistakes still lingering.

Kaina was washing glasses behind the bar. He was a tall, muscular man, strong enough to pull drunken sailors apart and deposit them out the back door. Yet he had such presence that the very fact of his body, his large hand resting lightly on someone's shoulder, was usually enough for people to leave of their own accord.

He quickly glanced behind Eva, at the door she'd just come through.

Checking to see if I'm being followed, Eva thought.

He nodded towards a stool, dried his hands on his apron, and stepped behind the small wooden bar to pour her a glass of beer. "I was told you might come here."

Eva nervously explained that she had found the dead man. "I think people are preventing me from finding out who he was."

Kaina looked interested. He said a name that did not mean anything to her. "As well, there is a missionary son gone missing, but I think he might just be running away from his family."

"The man I found was Hawaiian."

He had heard rumors of him as well. "Perhaps he is Kau, the young man who is up in the mountains fighting for the Queen, but probably not. That boy has nine lives."

"He was strangled," she said.

He poured himself a glass of water and leaned against the sink on the other side of the bar. "There are many ways to kill someone," he said.

They were both silent, sipping their drinks. Eva's fingers tore at the paper napkin beneath her glass.

She took a sip of beer.

"He is dead. You should let it go."

"I can't."

"Why not?" he asked, puzzled.

Because I am being watched, she thought. Because they think I know more than I do. And because by all rights that reward belongs to me. "A man dies and his body disappears. . . . I don't know, it simply isn't right."

Kaina drained his glass and set it down. "I have something to ask you. There is a message to be given to the Queen. Soon they will let some of her friends visit. It is arranged that meals will be taken to her. We are worried that otherwise the government might try to poison her. It helps that you are haole."

Visit the Queen? Step into that snakepit of soldiers and politicians? No, Eva thought, you have the wrong person. She held her hand up. "I can't possibly do it."

He raised his eyebrows.

"I am already being watched," Eva explained. "It would be far too risky."

"For who?" Kaina asked. "For you?"


*O*n the street outside the club, the children were playing a game with stones thrown into the middle of a circle of dirt. A girl about the same age as Malia landed a pebble in the center. She picked up another rock to throw, but at the last second she turned to Eva and held it out. She said something in Hawaiian and pointed towards the circle.

Eva rolled up her sleeve and took aim. Her rock landed within inches of the other, and the young girl spit into the dirt and nodded her approval.

The next rock thrown ricocheted off Eva's and crashed through the glass window of the photography studio across the street. The children scattered.

The door to the studio slammed open and a man ran into the street. He angrily asked Eva who'd thrown the rock into his window.

She held up her empty palms. "I have no idea."

"You were standing right here, and yet you have no idea." With the sole of his boot, he erased the circle drawn into the dirt, and kicked the rocks in different directions.

"I am as surprised as you are," Eva said, beginning to enjoy herself.

He went back into the studio and came out a moment later, dragging several pieces of wood.

"Hold up this end," he said. "At least you can do that."

Eva held the wood against the broken window, and the photographer cursed as he nailed the boards over the photographs of the haole leaders of the Republic.

"That's it," he muttered. "That's the problem. These photographs. That's why people are throwing rocks at my window. But politicians are the only people in town who can afford to have their picture taken."

"Yes," Eva said. "Stealing the Crown Lands hasn't hurt them financially."

He glanced at Eva. "Don't mistake me. I don't even like them myself. You ever notice their eyes, all glazed over? You see that in a fish, you know it's been dead too long to eat."

Eva nodded, amazed by his outburst.

As he finished covering the window, he turned and glared at her, then stepped inside and slammed the door behind him.

One side won and the other side lost. One side gave and the

other took, and it was important to be on the side of the takers. It was what she'd gone through life believing.

Now, staring down at the broken glass slowly disappearing into the mud, she felt confused. She walked slowly back to the club. Still time to turn around, she told herself as she pushed open the door.

Kaina was standing behind the bar.

Eva sat down and shook her head no when he asked if she wanted a beer.

"I'll pour you one anyway. In case someone comes. Why else go to a bar?"

"Yes, you're right. I am thirsty," Eva said.

Kaina set the beer down in front of her, and she nodded her thanks.

He leaned against the counter behind him. "Do you know the story of our King Kalakaua, Miss Hanson?"

She shook her head and took a sip of beer.

He divided a pile of napkins into thirds. "King Kalakaua. He was a good man, he was one of our best kings, did many good things. Kept the missionary businessmen in check. Kept them off balance, and that way he kept the monarchy alive. And still, the Bayonet Constitution. Forced to take away the voting rights of the majority of his people. And Pearl Harbor going to the Americans. There are some mistakes you can't recover from."

He looked up at Eva and she flushed, thinking of the jade necklace.

He shrugged. "Human nature."

"People make mistakes, they misjudge themselves. I wonder if Kalakaua knew how strong he really was. If you believe you have no power, then you act that way." He poured himself a beer and leaned against the bar. "You know how many Hawaiians own land?"

Eva stared down at the water-stained surface of the bar. "Less than five percent."

"Half of that, Eva. Half of five percent." He shook his head and set down the glass. "This is terrible beer, don't you think?"

"It's awful," she agreed.

He smiled. "But you know, the Americans like it."

Eva laughed.

"Who broke the window?"

"I don't know. I heard the glass breaking, but when I turned around, no one was there."

He stepped into the storeroom and reappeared with a sealed envelope. He placed it between them on the bar.

Eva's heart pounded as she picked it up and slipped it inside her boot.

"A basket of food will be brought to you. When you take it to the palace, the soldiers will search the basket, your purse, possibly more. Hide the note in your shoe. Better yet, those same boots."

He took her to the service entrance at the side of the club. "Too many visits through the front door doesn't look good," he said, as he unlocked the door and held it open.

"I'll see what I can find out about your dead man," he said. "And don't worry about the note. It's written in Hawaiian."

*D*uring her trial, Queen Liliʻuokalani was forced to defend herself against charges of treason.

How to define treason? In Hawaii, the very word was a stone thrown from a glass house. She was not allowed a jury of Hawaiian citizens. Instead, she was faced with a military jury.

Liliʻuokalani spoke of what the new government had done to her country. Those parts of her defense that reflected poorly on the Republic of Hawaii were ordered struck from the record.

Midway through her defense, the Queen switched from English to Hawaiian. Panic ensued. The trial was temporarily halted, until a translator could be found. No one in the court could speak more than a few words in Hawaiian.

The Queen won only this small victory.

# Twenty

*E*va stood at the window watching the butcher's sullen daughter coming towards her across the damp grass. "The butcher has been killing chickens," she announced.

Lehua looked up from her book, impressed with Eva's powers of divination.

Eva pointed out the window, at the girl with chicken feathers clinging to her muumuu and her hair.

"She's like a plucked angel," Lehua said.

"More like an unhappy wolf caught raiding the chicken coop."

The girl stepped inside and glared at them both. She walked past them into the kitchen and set down several packages of meat with blood leaking through the brown paper.

Eva was certain that the butcher soaked the meat in blood before he weighed it. There was no other explanation for such a quantity of blood. Whoever wanted to buy opium from him also had to buy his meat, and his daughter delivered both.

She set aside a small wrapped package of opium.

Lehua and Eva exchanged a look. Eva knew that her concern wouldn't change matters. Still, it was all she could do not to chase the girl out of the house, her and her bloody meat and her opium.

Lehua offered the girl a cup of guava juice. It pained Eva to see the way Lehua doted on the girl, even offering her a piece of cake.

As always, the girl refused, and then at the last moment she picked up the cake and ate quickly, like a person devouring her pleasure before she could experience it. She slammed down the plate and bolted through the door.

Lehua thought that the girl was afraid of Eva, worried that the haole fortuneteller could put harmful thoughts in her head.

As Eva mopped up the blood around the packages of meat, she wished that she could do such a thing, pour a hundred dark thoughts into the girl's head, send her off kicking and screaming.

And yet wasn't she too soon to be a deliverer of bad news? Even though the note she was to take to Queen Lili'uokalani was in Hawaiian, she hadn't dared to look at it. Could the message be anything but unfavorable?

In the afternoon, Eva made Lehua a plate of food and took it up to her bedroom. A mango sliced thin, a small piece of sweet potato, and toasted bread. Usually Lehua had no appetite after smoking opium, so Eva coaxed her with foods that were sweet and easy to swallow.

Under the mosquito net, Lehua's thin face rested against a pillow, her body under a white sheet. The Chinese herbalist had told Eva that you must always provide for ghosts, leave an offering for your ancestors. Eva thought that in Honolulu, with so many people pretending to be other than who they actually were, their ancestors must feel forsaken, and trail behind them like a vapor.

Lehua stirred a little and patted the side of the bed. Eva pulled the bedcovers over Lehua's feet and sat down next to her. "You should eat," she said.

Lehua shook her head.

She felt Lehua's forehead, expecting a fever, but her skin was cold and smooth as a stone. Lehua turned and faced the wall. A moment later, she was asleep.

Eva picked up the untouched plate of food and carried it downstairs. She stood for a long time in the empty kitchen, holding the plate in front of her, waiting for the weight pressing against her chest to lift.

*A* Hawaiian woman came to the back door, and Eva opened it without thinking. The woman held out a covered basket. "For the Queen," she said.

"Today?" Eva asked, confused. Kaina had given her the note only several days ago.

"Yes. Several days now, people are bringing her food. This is dinner. Go at five o'clock."

After the woman left, Eva took out the tarot cards. She shuffled and cut slowly, summoning her impressions of Queen Lili'uokalani, the smile at the corner of her mouth, her elegance, the way her fingers moved over her jet-bead necklace like a rosary when her thoughts were far away.

Eva picked only four cards, and set the deck aside. She turned the first card over. A young woman walked barefoot in the snow, leaving a trail of blood behind her. She looked at the card closely. Mormor must have enjoyed painting this one, she thought, with the globs of blood so theatrical, so overdone.

She set a second card above the first and turned it over. A piano floating in the sky.

Eva smiled. Mormor painted some cards as smoke screens. Breathers, she called them. A floating piano gave her time to think about the previous cards, or the hand of her customer, face up on the table in front of her. She'd turn that piano into anything at all. A pregnancy, a visitor, a hidden ambition.

What fun is the future, she'd said, if you can't meddle with it?

The third card up was a frog in a top hat, counting cash. No guesswork there, just those in charge adding up the profits. Green for greed, but envy as well.

She turned over the last card, one she'd painted herself after arriving on this island. A card full of water. Just a deep sea. No markers, no buoy, no lighthouse, no reef. No drowned man.

Lili'uokalani would be released, that's all she was certain of.

She checked the clock again, then quickly gathered up the cards and put them back in the suitcase.

$\mathcal{D}$ownstairs, she reached along the back shelf in the kitchen where she'd hidden Kaina's envelope. She unlaced a boot and slipped it inside. Lehua was still asleep when Eva left the house.

In the afternoon, the streets were busy. People clustered around the small smoking braisers, buying strips of char sui, meat sticks, and manapua wrapped in banana leaves. Everything was for sale, from chamber pots to aphrodisiacs, from ginger pomade to women.

Carrying the basket, Eva pushed her way through the crowd, worried that every part of her body was shaking, that all anyone had to do was take a good look at her to know everything about her, from the note hidden in her boot to the very first thing she'd ever stolen, a carved wooden horse that fit in the palm of her hand.

At the same time, another thought began. How was it that Kaina trusted her? He might trust this person she was becoming, but she didn't. So who was this, now taking a determined walk through Honolulu? Shut up, she told herself. Just keep walking.

She passed palm trees noisy with rats and protesting mynah birds, churches, and frowning missionary women in black dresses, the women that Lehua called bad weather approaching. It was true, they did look like strange black clouds heading down the sidewalks.

Rather than walk past them, Eva crossed the street. Under the shade of a large 'ulu tree, an impromptu hula lesson was taking place. Young girls danced and a woman accompanied them with an ipu heke 'ole, the open gourd played with the slap of a palm. The woman's voice was deep and resonant. The dancers' young hands moved together like a flock of birds, and their bodies seemed to grow lighter, their thin bones lifting up into the air. Eva was entranced.

The missionaries had so strongly disapproved of hula, seeing it as an immoral dance, that Ka'ahumanu, the widow of Kamehameha the Great, banned both hula and chanting after she had converted to Christianity. So a kapu was placed on hula, forcing people to dance in secret. When Queen Lili'uokalani's brother Kalakaua came to power, he brought the hula back, and it was said that several of the missionaries took to their beds in shock and never got up again.

When Eva reached the gates of Iolani Palace, she stopped in disbelief. Small campfires were burning on the lawn surrounding the palace, and soldiers circled the fires in small sweaty groups.

She stared at the tents and the careless fires and thought that it was true what people said about living near the equator. You were more likely to make snap decisions, to die of strange fevers, to fall in love with your opposite. The closer you came to zero latitude, the gaudier the birds, the more pungent the flowers, the more erratic the behavior, the quicker the heartbeat. It was like living with a fever, twenty-four hours a day.

It led a person to light fires in ninety degree heat.

She walked across the palace lawn, ignoring the soldiers' crude comments about her hair, the color of her skirt. A group of wilted people waited on the top steps of the palace, and she joined them. In the damp air, the women's fans fluttered like in-sects.

Finally, the doors were opened, and they were told to step through one at a time. Inside the palace, it was madness. Sol-diers and politicians crowded the rooms. Eva wondered if this was how the whole world was taken over, room by room, person by person.

A soldier took her basket and sifted through the contents. When he handed it back to her, he came closer and ran both hands down the sides of her skirt, the dirt from his palms leav-ing a stain like rust.

He made her take off her hat, looking at her suspiciously as he tapped against the lining.

As if there were a false bottom, Eva thought, and a flock of birds might emerge at any moment.

"I am a fortuneteller," she said, "not a magician."

Eva took the basket and moved towards a group of people huddled on chairs. She sat down next to a woman she recog-nized, though she didn't know whether she was a friend to Li-li'uokalani, or just someone who wanted something from her.

Perhaps she is wondering the same thing about me, Eva thought. And why am I here? For myself or for the Queen? Or perhaps for Kaina?

They all had their reasons for being there, she decided, and she didn't want to look too closely at her own.

The woman next to her held up a lottery ticket. "For luck," she said, but her nervous fingers had rubbed off the printed number. "That man," she whispered, "the dead man that was in the news-paper?" She dragged her chair closer. "I know who he was."

Her breath was hot on Eva's arm, and she clutched her arm with a hand as long and flat as a dried cuttlefish. Rhodes's words came back to her. When a man dies, everyone claims to have known him.

"He was a father, poor man. Left seven children behind." She sounded as certain of his identity as everyone else in Honolulu.

"He was a Royalist," she added in a louder voice.

Eva nodded, her eyes on a soldier who was admiring his new uniform in the mirror. He glanced in their direction and frowned.

"How long have you been waiting?" Eva asked after he looked away.

"About two hours," she said.

"Has anyone been allowed to see her?"

"Several people. Her maid. I've heard that they don't let her read anything except the Bible."

Eva glanced down at the woman's newspaper wrapped bouquet.

"I see you are bringing her food. I wouldn't put it past them to try poisoning her."

The clock beat out the hour and the row of visitors shifted, the women's crinolines sounding like surf breaking under their skirts.

Finally, Eva's name was called. As she picked up the basket, it shook in her hand. What was it Kaina told her? They are watching you for other reasons. It has nothing to do with the Queen.

"Go," the woman whispered, "before they change their minds."

She slowly walked up the wide stairs made from koa, the beautiful wood with sunlight trapped in it. Despite the beating the palace had gone through, it was still a beautiful building, as finely crafted as a boat.

At the top of the stairs another soldier pulled her aside. She panicked, thinking she would be searched again, this time more thoroughly. Instead, she was told to question Lili'uokalani about the guns.

Whose side could they possibly think I am on? she wondered. "Guns," she repeated stupidly.

"The guns that were dug up around her home. Get her to talk about them."

They underestimate Lili'uokalani, she thought, if they imagine she will say anything at all.

She was pointed towards the end of the hallway, where a maid stood with her arms full of clothing. A soldier ran his hands through the fabric, the slips, the underclothes, as if his hands were moving over a woman's body. He closed his eyes, feigning ecstasy. Another soldier laughed.

The Queen's clothing, Eva realized.

The maid pulled the clothes away, and the soldier stepped in front of the door, blocking her path.

"Move," she said, her foot shooting out and kicking hard into his shin.

He jumped backwards with a little shriek. A boy with more freckles than power.

"You shouldn't have done that." He took a step towards her, then noticed Eva and paused. The maid quickly opened a door and shut it behind her.

He picked up a ledger and told Eva to write her name in it.

She hesitated. Whose name should she use? The person she once was would have made her money and left town at the first hint of trouble.

She scanned the names quickly. One was Reverend Sereno Bishop, who often attacked Lili'uokalani in his Sunday sermons. Under the purpose for his visit, he'd written moral instruction.

They were letting in the people who hated her.

Eva signed her name and the soldier took back the book and glanced over her body. "You should tell my fortune sometime," he said.

Eva looked down at his hand. "You wouldn't want to hear it."

Outside Lili'uokalani's door, she took a deep breath and knocked on the wood with an unsteady hand.

There was no response. Eva looked over at the soldier.

"Go on in," he said.

Lili'uokalani stood at the far end of the room, as far away from the door as possible. She didn't turn around.

The room was a shock to see, stripped bare, with only a small wooden stool and a metal cot for her to sleep on. Eva had rescued her mother from debtors' prisons that were more accommodating.

As the door closed behind her, Eva realized she'd brought her own smell of fear into the room. She was drenched in it.

When the soldier resumed marching in the hallway, Lili'uokalani turned around.

"Ah, Miss Hanson." She had lost weight, and her face was lined with worry. She sat down on the cot, and motioned Eva towards the stool.

Eva curtsied, then handed her the basket of food.

Lili'uokalani lifted a warning finger to her mouth, hand cocked to her ear, and made a small walking gesture with her fingers.

While one soldier marched, another listened at the keyhole.

"I hope the guards have not bothered you," Lili'uokalani said.

"Not at all," Eva answered loudly, hoping to disappoint whoever was listening.

"They march twenty-four hours a day."

"How can you stand it?"

"Is there another choice?"

Eva quickly unlaced her boot and pulled out the note from Kaina.

Lili'uokalani slipped it under the edge of her sleeve. She would read it later.

While she laced her boot up, Eva quietly told Lili'uokalani that more of her friends had been arrested, that the government had sent soldiers up into the mountains to capture the Royalists who were still free.

Lili'uokalani nodded. She knew this already.

A moment later, the guard opened the door and Lili'uokalani

turned her face away. He announced that the visit was over. Eva looked at him in disbelief. She had been in the room less than five minutes.

He waited while Eva curtsied to the back of the Queen, and then he followed her out of the room. In the hallway, he asked if the Queen said anything about weapons, or the Royalists' plans.

"Don't be ridiculous," Eva said, her legs trembling. "My visit wasn't long enough for her to say anything at all."

Outside the palace, she passed one of the campfires burning on the grass. Without thinking, she picked up a soldier's jacket and threw it on the flames. It caught fire quickly and flared bright red, then collapsed like a day old hibiscus.

At the edge of the palace grounds, three blacksuited politicians observed her. They stared thoughtfully, patient as vultures waiting for a kill. Eva thought that for once one of her mother's cardinal rules was true. Bad news did travel in threes.

*I*t's not just in jail that all dreams are now of escape. Plantation owners dream of their childhood homes, while the Chinese dream of mountains so tall and beautiful that the sight of them is to be unsure of whether you are on earth or in heaven. The Japanese dream of rows of tea plants, of women with sleeves long enough to cast shadows on the ground. The missionaries dream that they are among the chosen on Noah's Ark, waiting for a world washed clean by God. The sailors dream of places they haven't yet seen, and the Hawaiians dream of Queen Lili'uokalani.

# Twenty-One

*T*hat evening, Eva and McClelland took the bicycle out and rode through the dark streets, with Eva propped up on the handlebars. They bounced over the rutted road, and she felt the strength in his legs, his breath warm and easy on the back of her neck.

An odd thought came to her. Remember how this feels. His breath, his arms around her.

"Are you cold?"

She shook her head no, trying to rid herself of the feeling that everything would end badly for the country. She thought of Queen Lili'uokalani locked in her small room. And Lehua's future? It was too depressing to contemplate.

They were headed for the harbor to watch the iceboat unload, so she tried to think about ice instead. How even the sound of it soothed, like a whisper.

They were so near the equator that ice had to be brought in on boats from places as far away as Alaska. The ice was bundled under thick blankets of burlap, and the boats raced against the heat and time that melted their profits.

McClelland told her that a crowd always gathered on the

dock just to watch the unloading, but Eva had spent far too much of her life around ice to believe him for a minute.

He avoided the main streets, instead taking the side roads that were well used. They passed crowds of people talking in careful groups, carrying small bundles, pulling wagons full of produce. The life of the town carrying on despite the restrictions.

When they reached the harbor, McClelland scanned the dock carefully, checking to see what each boat was unloading. Eva found herself doing the same.

With the roadblocks, it had become easier for people from the windward side of the island to bring their produce into Honolulu by boat, and the harbor was crowded with wooden canoes, dilapidated prams with patched sails, sampans that looked like they had been built from the wood of abandoned buildings.

Lantern light pooled in the water, and the rats were clearly visible, swimming between the boats.

The only thing holding still was the American warship, crouched in the water like the shadow of a large black dog. As the farmers worked, they glanced nervously at the boat every few minutes.

Merchants shouted orders as baskets of crabs and menpachi were unloaded. The fish were covered in limu, a thin layer of seaweed to keep them fresh.

A small boat bobbed like a rocking horse into the harbor. It was overloaded with produce, and the sides were barely two inches above water. In the stern a man rapidly bailed.

All eyes were on the boat, hoping it would last as far as the pier. The men left their own boats and quickly moved down to the edge of the dock, unloading the baskets of sweet potatoes and cabbage before the boat was even secured. The man at the stern continued bailing.

Soon after, a large ship with moon-brightened sails came into the harbor. Phosphorus surged across the bow, and a long gossamer skirt trailed behind the boat. It looked as if it wouldn't stop at all, that instead it would plow right through the wooden pier, the way things came at you in dreams.

McClelland turned to her and smiled. It was true, then, his story about ice. She slipped her hand into his.

Unloading ice was a complicated job due to its sheer weight, and the crew of hired men worked quickly through the night, racing against the sun which right then was tipping over Europe and coloring the eastern edge of the Atlantic Ocean.

Halfway through the shift, they took a break. The men bent from the waist and swung their arms, stretched out on the ground and pulled their knees up to their chests to loosen their spine. They drank cups of hot tea or sipped furtively from a bottle of rum.

A man in thick worker's clothing walked past, pausing to fumble with matches and a cigarette until he caught McClelland's eye. McClelland nodded, and Eva felt his body stiffen. The man threw the cigarette into the water and walked off into the shadows.

A moment later, a wagonload of soldiers appeared at the end of the dock.

Eva stood up to run, but McClelland pulled her back down. "No, sit. You'll bring less notice if you don't move."

The soldiers began searching the boats, not telling anyone what they were looking for, just calling it an inspection.

"Since when we need inspection?" an angry fisherman called out.

"Since now," a soldier with a gun answered.

They prodded through the piles of vegetables with long sticks, and ordered large bolts of fabric to be unrolled across the dock.

A soldier tipped over a basket and fish sprayed out along the dock and spilled over into the water.

"I don't believe this," Eva said, turning to McClelland.

*The Floating City · 203*

He wasn't there.

Her gaze ran along the end of the pier, and then among the boats, but he had completely disappeared. She buttoned her jacket, trying to make herself less noticeable.

The search continued through the boats and the stacks of produce grew on the pier, but all the soldiers were coming up with was Chinese cabbage and hostility.

Eva sat on the dock, pretending that she didn't mind the sight of soldiers tearing apart farmers' baskets and trampling their produce. They glanced at her, curious to see a haole woman on the dock. As the farmers quickly moved off the dock, she realized it was unsafe to remain where she was.

She picked up her bicycle and wove her way into the middle of the farmers leaving the harbor. As she passed the iceboat, one of the men called to her, holding up a small block of ice.

"Go down towards Chinatown," he whispered, handing her the ice. She set it in the basket on the back of the bicycle and loudly thanked him for the ice.

The soldiers and farmers were now yelling back and forth, and she was relieved by the diversion. At the end of the street, she turned and rode towards Chinatown. She passed men smoking in the dark, and a card game played around a lantern. The slap of the cards echoed on the empty street. She had the feeling that everything had long since been decided, and whoever held the winning hand simply hadn't shown it yet.

A man ran towards her. "It's me," McClelland called softly.

"Where did you go?" she asked. "I was worried."

"I'm sorry, Eva. So many soldiers . . ." he trailed off.

This was the wrong night, she thought. What he was waiting for hadn't yet arrived. Were all those people watching the iceboat actually waiting for more guns?

"What is this about?" she asked.

"Probably just an inspection," he answered, clearly unwilling to say more.

As they rode back to his house, Eva told him one of her mother's stories of a girl who snuck out of her house to go ice-skating in the middle of the night. As she moved over the ice, she turned into different creatures—a wolf with fur bursting from around her wrists and neck, then a swan with beautiful wings. As she moved farther from the shore, she decided to see what being a bear would be like, but by then she had skated to the thin middle of the pond, and the ice couldn't hold the weight of the bear. Cracks darted out from under her feet. Before she could turn into something else, she sank beneath the ice and died.

There are times when nothing can save you.

The sun was up when she rode home from McClelland's cottage, and as she pedaled through the warm morning air she found herself suddenly homesick for the sound of someone skating across ice, even homesick for one of her mother's terrible stories.

She tiptoed into Lehua's kitchen holding the ice with both hands, as if it were the crown of her lost country. She put it in the wooden icebox and went upstairs to sleep, knowing that by the time she woke up it would just be ice.

*he English language newspapers stepped up their campaign against Queen Lili'uokalani. Each lie was more lurid than the previous. Sorcery, black magic, the sacrifice of household pets. An article accusing the Queen of eating small black puppies was the morning's front page headline.*

*Another article claimed that Lili'uokalani and her brother Kalakaua were the illegitimate offspring of a black coachman. Missionaries asked their haole congregations to join together to ensure that all Hawaiian children continue to be kept out of their schools.*

# Twenty-Two

*I*t stormed the entire next day, but by evening the rain had ended, and it was so quiet that the ocean could be heard. People stopped what they were doing and went outdoors to listen to the waves.

Eva was outside as well, sitting on the steps of the lanai and fingering a note Lehua had left her. She'd read it four times over but still wasn't grasping the three words written down. *Gone to Molokai,* the note read. To the leper colony.

Eva had seen lepers in Europe, wearing the large scarlet L sewn onto their clothes, and ringing a bell to warn people of their presence. Lehua had told her that before Father Damien came to Molokai the lepers were kept behind fences, like cattle. Damien took down the fences and lived with the people. The American missionaries mistrusted him. He was French, and worse than that, Roman Catholic. Lili'uokalani had visited the colony and formed an unlikely friendship with the priest. Like him, she was not scared to move among the lepers, to break bread with people who no longer had hands.

What would Lehua find on Molokai? If her mother was still alive, would she even recognize her under the ravages of disease?

Eva nervously fingered the piece of paper, wearing it down to the softness of fabric.

She listened to the sea and an occasional high shrieking sound that took her a moment to realize was just the Widow sharpening her new machete. A dog began to bark at the end of the road, and there were footsteps coming up the path to the house.

Cornelius Rhodes walked up to the lanai and stood in front of Eva, staring down at her.

When the full moon was visible, Lehua called it kau ka mahina. A bald man appears. So, what would she call this? Eva wondered.

When bad luck takes up residence in a hand, there is nothing that can be done about it. So here was Rhodes, his gelatinous skin slick on this hot night. She thought that if she pushed a stick into him it would go right through to the other side.

"Good evening, Miss Hanson."

Eva tucked the note into her pocket and didn't answer.

He mopped his face with a handkerchief that was already far too damp for the task. Even the tight collar of his shirt was damp with sweat. "I will come right to the point."

She looked at him with a mixture of fear and disgust. Could he have found out about the note she'd passed on to the Queen? Or was this somehow about Lehua? Had the boat sunk? Was she never coming back from Molokai?

"You have specifically been told to stop making pills with false claims."

"But I have stopped," she said, relieved.

His face was blank.

"I have stopped," she repeated.

He sighed, and glanced at the sagging porch, the chicken coop leaning against the side of the house.

He leaned forward, taking hold of her arm. "Miss Hanson. By now, you must be aware that I find out everything that happens on this island. Everything."

She pulled her arm and his grasp tightened. As his face came closer, she smelled whiskey on his breath.

"What is it you've found out?" he said.

"I have no idea what you're talking about."

"You know exactly what I'm talking about."

"Let go of me," she said, and was surprised when he did.


$\mathcal{A}$ faint trade wind blew as Eva walked quickly through Honolulu, with no destination in mind, just fueled by her own panic. Around her, the sound of the ocean steadily rose. The same sound, she thought, that Lehua was listening to right now.

Rhodes wanted to know what she'd found out. Nothing, really. She hadn't yet heard back from Kaina, and she was no closer to knowing about the dead man than before.

The wind carried the sound of a muffled argument, drunken sailors fighting over what they always fought over: women and money, the fear that their real life was taking place somewhere else and they were missing it.

A soldier staggered past, holding a whiskey bottle in front of him like a divining rod. He loudly threatened to tear out the long hair of any Chinese man he ran into.

Along the wall, the night blooming cereus had opened, flowers that reminded Eva of the discarded gloves that women used to leave in charity bundles for the poor. Yellowed, full of holes, and shrunken too small for her long fingers. The gloves she'd grown up wearing.

A man with a load on his back ran past, and Eva stepped into the shadows along Beretania Street. At Iolani Palace, the new electric lights were lit along the front of the building, but the upstairs window where the Queen was held was dark. Not even a blade of light leaked through the wooden shutters.

Eva stared up at the shutters. What was there to see in that dark room? Lili'uokalani's graceful hands counting a string of beads in her hand, each bead slipping past, another second, another minute. What could she be planning? Even if she could escape, where was there for her to go?

Across the road, the statue of King Kamehameha loomed out of the darkness. Kamehameha the Great, the unifier of all the islands. The first statue of Kamehameha fell overboard on the sea voyage to Hawaii. Some said it had been scavenged and set up in a seaport in Argentina, while others claimed that it was still in the Pacific Ocean, but even at the bottom of the sea the currents pulled and twisted. The first Kamehameha could have traveled halfway around the world by now.

Tonight, all of Honolulu felt submerged, as if they had joined Kamehameha at the bottom of the sea, their lives as fragile as coral, as memorable as the fishes.

A sudden wind rattled the palm fronds like dice in a cup. Eva flattened herself against the wall as an old man holding a machete limped past, the blade glinting like a cat's eye.

At the end of the block was the herbalist's shop, and she was relieved to see a light on in the window. She ducked through the low doorway and was surrounded by a pungent smell that was half sea and half land.

The herbalist sat on a high stool, beckoning Eva forward. Behind him the wall was filled with small wooden drawers, each labeled in careful Chinese script.

The promise in each drawer was why Eva came. The dried snake, the cartilage of a stingray, the rows of small bottles with infusions of leaves from places as far away as Singapore and Thailand.

He sold her powders that they both hoped would take away Lehua's desire for opium. Eva secretly stirred the powders into Lehua's tea, rum, guava juice. Who knew what would help? Addiction wasn't something visible, something you could watch lessening.

Eva told him that Lehua had gone to Molokai.

He nodded, not surprised.

"You knew that she was planning this?"

He shrugged. "These things are never planned, are they?"

Eva took a deep breath and sat down.

"I've been to Molokai," he said. "It's a sad place, yes. Better now, after Father Damien. Before that, many people swam out to sea rather than spend their lives in the leper colony."

"I am worried about her," Eva said.

"Yes. But Molokai is not far. Let me show you something."

He handed Eva a bone and asked her to guess what it was. She held it up to the light. The bone was long and delicate, the edge of it almost translucent, like a fingernail.

She shook her head. She had no idea.

Think how far this bird must have traveled, he told her. Even a butterfly can travel thousands of miles, with wings no stronger than paper.

He took the bone and carefully set it down on the counter. "Lehua is like this bird," he said.

Maybe so, she thought. Maybe not. He picked up a wooden letter opener and smelled it, then handed it to Eva.

"Smells like dust," Eva said, and he laughed. He dipped a cloth in water and ran it over the wood. "Now smell."

"Sandalwood," she guessed.

He nodded, placing the wood alongside the bone. "Many people died for this smell. This wood." He told her that when his father was little he had a job cutting down the brush around the sandalwood trees, in preparation for the men to cut the tall trees down. A small boy with a machete. People didn't know any better. All the wood was sent to China. Not one tree left standing, not if the Hawaiian people didn't want to get in trouble with their ali'i.

The chiefs took all the money, this was back in 1815. The people had nothing to eat, they were starving, but the ali'i became rich in the Chinese market at Canton. Kamehameha the Great realized what was happening and put a kapu on the sandalwood, so that people would go back to farming. But after his death his son lifted the kapu, and the trade continued.

His father had traveled on a boat loaded with sandalwood, all the way to Canton. No one paid him, and he was stuck in Canton for at least a year. Yet, when he finally came home, he brought back a Chinese wife. The herbalist smiled. "My mother." He set the wood down next to the bone. "Sometimes good can come out of much misery."

He gave Eva more powders for Lehua, folded into small paper envelopes. After she paid, he locked the shop door behind her.

Eva wandered past the noisy sailors' bars, the tattoo parlors, the shops still open, selling yukata fabric for summertime kimonos. Even at night, there were baskets of ginseng root spilling out into the streets, and rows of dried squid hanging like bats from thin bamboo poles.

In the shadows, a group of men were quickly unloading large wooden boxes from the back of a horse drawn wagon, then carrying them through a dark doorway.

They were far too quiet to be soldiers.

A man stepped forward to calm the horse as a lantern was brought out of the warehouse. The light swept across the back of the empty wagon and the faces of the men, and she saw Jonathan standing in the back.

A moment later, the driver swung himself into the front of the wagon. Jonathan stepped off the back and talked to the driver for a moment, then disappeared into one of the warehouses.

Eva held her breath and backed away.

The driver made a soft clicking noise and blew out his lamp. The horse slowly pulled the wagon down the road. Eva moved quickly in the opposite direction.

*After the capture of the Royalists, Honolulu turned into a carnival of words, with a different barker on every corner. Crowds gathered nightly outside the palace grounds. Some claimed that England would step in and rescue Hawaii from the Americans. Torch waving evangelicals declared that the wrath of God was descending and the islands would soon sink down into the sea unless the wishes of the Americans were embraced.*

*On the second floor of the palace, Queen Lili'uokalani paced through the dark room, from the wall to the sleeping cot to the washstand to the barred window, never once touching anything at all.*

# Twenty-Three

*A* woman stood in the front yard, staring at a piece of paper clutched in her hand. Eva stepped outside and greeted her, but the woman didn't answer. She handed Eva a slip of paper with her address on it.

Eva ushered her around the side of the house to the small room at the back. Once indoors, the woman made no attempt to remove her thick veil.

If you had nothing to hide, then what did you have? She suspected the woman had come to her over an affair of the heart. She was tired of telling women to follow their hearts, tired of hearing about unhappy love affairs. Yes, of course it led to trouble. It was your heart after all, not a guide in lederhosen who had memorized the trail.

Or perhaps she wanted news of Queen Lili'uokalani. If so, Eva knew nothing more than anyone else. She shuffled the tarot deck and set the cards down on the table between them, realizing that the woman had no interest in the cards.

Eva looked for a particular gesture, a fluttering eyelid, a hesitation, but the woman gave nothing away.

Eva asked if she wanted word of the future, or perhaps to contact the dead?

When the woman finally spoke, it was in English too perfect to be her first language. A first language is a child bursting into the room, too exuberant to care what is knocked over or ripped apart. Every language after that moves with the cautious step of an adult.

She said her name was Alexandra. "I wish to find out about the man whose body was found in the canal in Waikiki."

Eva caught her breath.

As the woman spoke, she took off her hat and lifted the veil. She looked Mongolian, with high cheekbones and the shape of her eye as beautiful as a curved knife.

"What sort of information are you looking for?"

"I am curious to know why the English newspapers are lying."

"It's more surprising when they tell the truth," Eva answered.

Alexandra placed her hand on the table, a hand narrow as a river fish. "I have heard that you are the person who found him."

What if she has come from Rhodes, Eva thought. "Where would you hear something like that?"

Alexandra shook her head, and pulled out a small muslin bag of the sort that banks used for carrying money. Coins clinked together as she set it on the table.

"This information is only for myself." She glanced up at Eva. "I will tell no one else."

When people reassure you that they won't say a word to anyone, Eva thought, it's always the first thing they'll do.

"Who are you here for, in addition to yourself," Eva asked, as gently as she could.

Alexandra looked down for a moment, then nodded. "A woman," she said softly, "a woman who knew him. If we are speaking of the same man."

"Why doesn't she come to see me?"

"She can't."

"Why not?"

"She is afraid."

Eva thought of the man's well made clothing, the country style shirt. "You know more about this than I do."

The woman shook her head, denying it.

"I understand how you feel," Eva said. "We all have reasons to be cautious."

"It isn't his life that she wants to know about, but his death. We were sent to you by Kaina."

Eva nodded, relieved. "I'll tell you what I know, but I should speak directly to her."

"She is waiting outside in the carriage," Alexandra said. "I will try to convince her."

Eva watched her walk quickly down the path. It was almost too dark to see outside, the sky streaked like an old mirror.

The money was still on the table. Eva picked up the muslin bag and felt the weight. It was substantial.

From behind the cupboard, she took out the box holding the jade necklace. She opened it, ran her finger lightly over the jade, as green as a butterfly cocoon.

A woman took off her necklace and wrapped it around a man's wrist. A lover's gesture, playful. Then he wore it through the day to remind him of her. Yet what had happened after that? What had occurred between the necklace and the rope burn around his neck?

There was a soft knock on the door. As Eva opened it, Alexandra stepped aside and gestured to a woman standing behind her. She was Japanese, with thick black hair and the kind of skin that pulled the light to it.

Eva asked her to sit down. The woman spoke quickly in Japanese. Alexandra stood behind her, translating into English.

Her eyes were red rimmed, her features delicate. She had

beautiful hands, but her nails were bitten down to the quick, which made Eva guess that she was younger than she appeared in her fine kimono. It also made Eva trust her.

The Japanese woman told Eva she was the wife of the man in question.

Eva was filled with dread. "I'm so sorry," she said, glancing up at up at Alexandra, who nodded.

"I found him," Eva said.

As Alexandra translated, the woman shook her head from side to side.

"Not in the canal. Not like the papers reported."

The woman curled her hands into fists.

"It was several miles outside Honolulu, down at a cove where the fishing is good. I went for a walk along the shoreline and came to a cluster of rocks. Out where the waves break." There was no reason to mention anyone else. "I found him there."

She tied that necklace around the wrist of her husband, Eva thought. She saw the woman smoothing his long hair off his face. She saw them laughing together.

"What was he wearing?" Alexandra asked.

"He was barefoot. Long pants, dark blue, and a white shirt made from raw silk."

Eva looked at Alexandra. "Was he a Royalist?" she asked softly.

"He was sympathetic to the Queen. His business was with the people, though, not the monarchy."

"What kind of business?"

"He was a farmer. He was trying to prevent the Americans from purchasing all of the land and turning it into cane fields. But now we are confused."

Alexandra gestured to the other woman. "She has been forced off her land, out of her home, because her husband sold everything. The land, farms. Even their house. We don't know why. She was told that he'd gone to the United States."

She gestured towards the crying woman. "She thought he didn't love her anymore."

It wasn't fair, but then what was? Eva tried to push it aside, but the woman's plight affected her. She was alone, certainly, but there must be someone left to look after her. She was still wearing fine clothing.

Then Eva thought of her mother, selling her long coat, her gold earrings. She'd tried to turn the visits to the pawnshop into a game, so that Eva wouldn't realize how desperate their situation actually was.

Eva turned and reached for the box. "And there was this," she said, holding up the jade.

The woman's breath came in a soft gasp. Her hand moved timidly towards the necklace, but didn't touch it. She started crying.

Alexandra asked if the police had seen the necklace.

"No one has seen it," Eva said. Except Lehua and the jeweler.

When the woman stood up, Eva handed her the box.

She was startled, and spoke hurriedly in Japanese as she slipped the box into the sleeve of her kimono.

Eva thought that if her mother had known about clothing like this, deep sleeves that could hide whatever they were pickpocketing, she would have moved them to Japan.

"Kalama," Alexandra said. "She wants you to know his name. Kalama."

"Kalama," Eva repeated, seeing again the thick wet hair that covered the man's face.

Alexandra picked up the bag of money and handed it to Eva.

"No," Eva murmured. She couldn't believe what she'd just done. For the first time in her life she had refused money. She pulled her jacket closer. A fever, she decided, I must be coming down with a fever.

The women talked privately for a moment. Then the Japanese woman nodded and reached into the sleeve of her kimono. She held out a small object tied to a long silk cord.

"Do you know what this is?" Alexandra asked.

"It's netsuke," Eva said, admiring the detailed carving. A very small rabbit sitting up on its haunches. She knew about netsuke because Tomas had an obsession with scrimshaw, with anything carved.

"Is it ivory?"

The two women spoke for a moment, and Alexandra nodded. "From the eighteenth century. She's owned it for a very long time. She wants you to have it."

The Japanese woman stepped close to her and placed it in Eva's palm, then gently closed Eva's fingers over it. It was the size of a kukui nut. Eva opened her hand and looked at it carefully. Up close, the rabbit was smiling.


After they left, Eva absentmindedly rearranged the objects in front of her. A piece of coral. A small koa bowl. She placed the netsuke rabbit in the center of the table.

Kalama was dead, and his widow was forced from her home. She wrapped the silk cord around the carved animal until it disappeared.

The woman would pawn the jade, Eva realized. And not get enough money for it. Then she'd have to sell off her beautiful kimonos and whatever else she'd managed to hang onto so far.

Who had helped her mother? No one. Just a bad luck handful of men, all of whom cost more than they gave.

If she knew exactly how Kalama had lost his land, she might be able to help his widow and find out who was responsible for his death. If she could, she'd have traced the last days of Kalama's life, but that path had disappeared along with his body.

It was time for her to visit the land office and see what she could find out on her own.

The clerk behind the counter in the land records office looked like what was left after the tide went out. Old bones and pinkish, peeling skin and faded hair.

When Eva asked if he had a list of recent real estate sales, his eyes blinked like a turtle's, but he didn't answer.

She repeated her request.

He grunted irritably and slipped off his stool. His fingers traced over the rows of books on the shelf behind him, and stopped at a dark red ledger. He pulled it from the shelf and placed it on the counter in front of Eva.

She opened it and scanned several pages. It was the listing for land transactions for the island of Kauai.

"No, I am interested in land sales for this island. For Oahu."

He chose another ledger from the shelf and handed it to her. It was the right island but the wrong year.

"These listings are several years old. Perhaps I am not making myself clear. I'm looking for current sales."

He shook his head.

"Pardon?"

"We haven't any of those."

"You're saying that you don't have records of current sales?"

"Exactly."

She glanced up at the bookshelf, clearly seeing the red spines of the ledgers, with the dates stamped in gold. She could have told the clerk that they were right there behind him, but his manner warned her against it.

"Do you have a name or a particular purchase you wish to find out about?"

That was it. He wanted names, wanted to know who she was looking for. She pretended to look through her purse. "I thought I had it written down. I'll have to come back another time."

Outside the land office, Eva wanted to run, but forced herself to walk slowly down the street, feeling the eyes of the clerk still upon her. Someone didn't want people knowing what was taking place up in Nuuanu Valley.

As she turned the corner, she ran into Betty, one of the wealthiest women in Honolulu, with her arm hooked into Edward's. Betty was a superstitious woman who had sent a lot of business her way.

After meeting Betty on the beach that day she had met Queen Lili'uokalani, Eva held an occasional afternoon séance at Betty's house. It was an easy job. A room full of women with unfulfilled desires, and the air crackling like just before an electrical storm.

If Edward had his sights on Betty, he was doing better than Eva had realized. He was smoking a cheroot, a satisfied look on his face.

The subject of the Queen's imprisonment came up, and Betty waved her hand dismissively. "Well, it's a temporary situation, I'm sure."

"But this is her country."

Edward frowned at Eva, shook his head in a warning.

"Your sympathies must lie with the Royalists," Betty said in a disapproving voice.

Eva turned her back on the two of them and quickly walked away. She listened to her heels click like coins dropping against the sidewalk. In Honolulu, there were spacious sidewalks for the rich parts of town, planks slapped across the dirt for the poor. With each step, she added up the money she'd no longer make off Betty.

That was stupid, she told herself. First I don't accept the money from the Japanese woman, and now I've insulted my best customer. What has come over me? I'm not turning into some sort of goody-goody, am I?

Goody-goody. Lehua called it ho'omikanele, acting like a missionary.

*A* rumor circulated that the Americans were planning to put the Hawaiian people onto reservations, the way they had done to the native Indian people in their own country. The massacre at Wounded Knee had occurred only several years earlier, in 1890, and the fate of the Sioux Indians was seen as a warning that it could happen here.

# Twenty-Four

$\mathcal{I}$n the middle of the night, the door to Eva's bedroom opened. "Jonathan?" she asked.

Lehua's laugh filled the room. "Is he still calling himself that?" She sat down on the edge of the bed.

Eva reached out in the dark, felt Lehua's thin arm. Good, she thought, not a ghost. Lehua had been gone a week, and Eva wanted both to throw her arms around her and to scream at her. She did neither.

Lehua fumbled for the matches and tried to light the lamp. After the third match went out, Eva took the box from her and lit the lamp.

Lehua's face was damp with sweat. "Are you all right?" she asked.

Lehua jumped to her feet. "Tonight I am going to teach you to dance hula."

Eva shook her head. She didn't want to learn hula, she wanted to know what had happened on Molokai.

"A simple hula," Lehua coaxed. "The very first one my mother taught me. Come, stand up, put your hands like this," she said, moving too quickly, her hands jerking from side to side.

"Lehua. You need to calm down."

"Why?" Her eyes glittered in the light.

"What has happened? Are you all right?"

Lehua ignored her questions. "Here is a fact. You like facts, Eva. Don't all haoles collect facts when they come to a country like ours? How much rainfall, how many goats. But here's something you don't know. After the missionaries outlawed hula, people would see a missionary walking past and they would hum a hula." Lehua laughed. "Their way of telling the missionaries to go to hell. But Hawaiians didn't believe in hell, did you know that, Eva? Only the haoles could think up something that terrible."

"Lehua, you should rest."

"Hele mai," Lehua said, "I want to be outside."

Eva followed her downstairs. They found an umbrella on the lanai and went out into the rain.

The street disappeared into mud and covered their feet. They gave up on the umbrella and walked bareheaded.

Soldiers often bothered women out at night, but the rain had emptied the roads, the business of Honolulu taking place indoors.

Lehua turned up a small dirt path and stopped in front of an old cottage. Around them was the sharp scent of guavas left to rot in the grass and wood gone moldy.

She wiped the dirt off a small window and peered in. Eva did the same.

"It looks abandoned," Eva said.

Lehua didn't answer. She pulled down a vine growing against the side of the house.

"Why isn't anyone living here?" Eva asked.

Lehua pulled down another vine, her fingers scratching the wood.

Eva took hold of her hand and led her over to the lanai.

"Sit down," she said, and Lehua complied. "Who owns this house?"

The rain leaked down through the rotting eaves. Eva sat next to her, and Lehua opened her umbrella over them both.

"I own this hale," Lehua finally said. "It was my mother's house."

"Ah." Eva was worried to hear what was coming next.

"My mother. She didn't know who I was, Eva. But I recognized her."

"That's good."

"I should have gone to see her before now," Lehua whispered. "But I was scared. Scared of what I would find."

"It's good that you went."

"There was a priest on Molokai who told me what had happened to her. I never knew anything more than what my father said about her, which wasn't much."

Lehua explained that her mother's leprosy started as a small lump the size of a fish eye. And while she was trying to figure out what to do next, her father saw it and decided for them both. He didn't say anything to her about it, and she thought she understood that silence to mean that the two of them would keep it hidden.

He waited until she went out fishing one morning and he packed up the whole house and disappeared, taking Lehua with him.

Her mother came home to an empty house, with just a sheet left on the sleeping pallet because he was worried it might be diseased. He was less worried about the small tin canister she kept her money in, taking it with him. She was lucky she had her fishing gear with her or he would have taken that, too.

The neighbors wondered why her husband had left so quickly, without even a fight. She told them that he was in love with another woman, and they believed it so readily that her feelings were hurt.

Yet, when the sores on her foot became worse and she never took the bandage off, her face no longer existed, they only looked at her foot. She said that she had cut it on a piece of coral out fishing on the reef, but no one believed her.

Finally, someone gave her name to the leper catchers, and they came one night to her back door. She ran out the front, down into a field of wetland taro. She crouched in the muddy water, near a water buffalo with pale horns curved like a fish-hook.

The leper catchers splashed and cursed, while the water buffalo stood still as a mountain for her to hide behind. They finally went mauka, towards the mountains, so she ran makai, towards the sea.

"Then what happened to her?" Eva asked softly.

Her mother spent six months living like a dog, hiding in the mountains during the day, coming out for food at night. Finally, they caught her down near the harbor. She couldn't have run if she'd wanted to, not since the leprosy had taken hold of her foot and twisted it into a rag.

She was put on a boat heading for Molokai, along with other captured lepers. They were taken away at night, as if the sight of Oahu turning its back on them would be too painful to bear in daylight.

It was at night to cover the leper catchers' own shame, Eva thought, putting her arm around Lehua's thin shoulders.

They sat quietly, listening to the rain hitting the umbrella, the damp fabric that smelled like the inside of a circus tent.

Eva wanted to give Lehua something in return. But what could she say that Lehua would want to hear? Perhaps her real name, but it was a sound that had stayed lodged in her throat for too long.

"I've taken someone else's name," she finally said. "Stolen it, actually."

"Hanai," Lehua said. "It's called hanai. Borrowing, not taking." She spun the umbrella, and the rainwater flew out around them like a layer of glass.

$\mathcal{A}$t home, Lehua pushed open the front door, and Eva noticed something sticking out of the mail slot. She leaned down, taking a closer look. It was a piece of drying meat. More meat had been pushed through the slot.

She turned, silently asking Lehua.

"It's the butcher," Lehua said, sleepily.

"What about the butcher?"

"You know what he's like. Meat along with the opium. I haven't been buying anything from him, and he's angry."

"So he's threatening you with rotten meat?"

"It's been going on for some time now. He does the same thing to other people, too."

The next morning, they scraped the meat off the floor and pulled the last piece through the mail slot. Eva put it all in a bag and headed out the door.

In the front yard of the orphanage, Malia watched Eva with golden eyes, the color that hardened lava sometimes took on. She showed Eva the flute she had carved from the long stem of a papaya leaf, the finger holes bored with a small knife.

"Tomas gave me his pocketknife," she bragged. "He told me promise I don't cut myself."

"And did you?"

"Oh, yes," she said, laughing. "I promise." She held out her finger. "And then I cut myself. But I need this knife, if the Queen needs my help to escape."

Eva nodded, as if a child brandishing a knife were a regular sight. She asked Malia to play a song on the new flute, but the girl shook her head. "A man stay watching your house," she said.

"What kind of man?" Eva asked, thinking first of Jonathan, then Rhodes. "Do you remember what he looked like?"

"A haole in black clothes," Malia whispered. "I see him two times now."

"Did he have a big white face, sort of soft looking?"

Malia shrugged. "They all do, yeah?" She grabbed the front of her muumuu and crumpled the fabric in her fist. "He looks mean," she added.

"He is mean," Eva agreed.

"It's a war, yeah?"

"Yes, it is. It just doesn't look like one."

Malia nodded solemnly. "What's in your bag?" she asked.

"Rotten meat."

"You stay kidding, right?"

*T*he afternoon was so hot that when the churchbells rang nothing answered. Even the dogs were silent, hiding under houses or shade trees.

As the temperature rose, a tin roof buckled in the heat with a sound like gunfire. Carrying the bag of meat, Eva passed a sturdy woman who walked with sea legs, and a tired man with a freckled hand of bananas across his back like a bright yellow cloak. Another man played a harmonica, his foot keeping time in the dirt. Around him several children edged closer to the strange instrument, their delight outweighing their shyness.

The butcher's daughter was plucking chickens out in front of the shop, white feathers flying up around her like the sails of a boat going nowhere. She was startled to see Eva, and quickly looked away.

Inside the shop, the butcher was leaning against the dirty counter. Behind him, long strips of flypaper were blackened with dead flies.

Eva set the sack of meat down on the counter.

"What's dis?" he asked.

"Meat."

"You bringing me meat?" He smiled, and his teeth were far too white. He should have teeth the color of veal, she thought.

"This is the meat you've been pushing through our mail slot. I want it to stop."

"You the haole fortuneteller, yeah? Living at Lehua's house," he said. It sounded like an accusation.

Eva opened the sack and dumped the meat out on the counter. "Stay away from us," she said.

"Or else what? You going give me the evil eye? Who you tink is scared of you?" he asked. "You the one should be scared. You the one they stay watching."

He was still smiling when she left the shop.

Outside, the girl turned her face away.

*A*s Eva walked down the street, a wave of anger came over her. In the crowd, she saw the thin hair of the land office clerk. He went into a private club, and she stepped up to the window and watched him talking to a waiter. A moment later, he was led into the dining room.

She turned back to the street where the land office was located, knowing it was exactly what she shouldn't be doing. Her nature was to disappear at the first sight of trouble. Further involvement would only make her life more difficult.

She opened the door on a young clerk eating a sandwich, his waxed mustache wiggling like a pair of chopsticks.

He colored slightly and pushed his lunch out of view. "May I help you?"

Eva asked to see the list of current real estate transactions.

"Certainly," he said, turning to the shelf behind him. He searched through the ledgers. "Well, that's odd. They should be right here. Let me look in the back."

He was gone for a long time. Eva paced back and forth, hoping the other clerk was planning on a long lunch.

Finally, he came back carrying an armful of red ledgers. "We're usually much more organized than this," he apologized, setting the books down on the counter.

"Now, what year are you interested in?"

"The present," she said.

"Here we are." He flipped a ledger open to the most recent entries and handed it across the counter to her. He gave her a ruler and showed her how to run it down the page.

The list of current sales took up many pages, mostly consisting of houses sold in Honolulu and in the outlying areas. Eva quickly skimmed down the lists, looking for sales of land and wondering how much time she had before the head clerk reappeared. The names of missionary families appeared over and over again, which didn't surprise Eva, after what Edward had told her.

She found Kalama's name listed as the seller of seventy acres of land up in Nuuanu Valley. The selling price was so low she thought it must be a mistake.

Then she saw something that stopped her completely.

Cornelius Rhodes was listed as the buyer of the land. She read his name twice, too shocked to believe it the first time. Rhodes was listed as the buyer of several other pieces of land, all of them remarkably inexpensive. All bought from the same man, Kalama.

She pointed it out to the clerk.

He whistled over the price. "Now, that is a bargain," he agreed.

"How would this occur?"

"Well, possibly a disagreement among the heirs, or a family fallen on hard times, which happens often with farmers. Someone might even be convinced that the land was haunted."

"Haunted?"

"I've heard of that happening," he shrugged, but he was clearly as puzzled as Eva.

"What does this code mean, under the listings?"

"That's actually the selling date, but for some reason they've put the months as letters." He laughed. "Someone's idea of how to confuse things. So, you see, January is A, February is B."

Eva felt her bones turn to water. Kalama was dead before any of these land transactions. He died before he could have sold the land to Rhodes.

What was it Lehua had told her that day on the beach, when they found the dead man? Measles and venereal disease are too slow. Now they are murdering us, she'd said.

So that was why Rhodes was after her. He thought that she already knew that Kalama had died before these dates.

And yet she couldn't prove anything. The word of a fortuneteller wouldn't hold up in court.

Kaina, she thought suddenly. She'd take the information to him. He'd know what to do. She quickly jotted down the dates and the property sold. Her hand shook as she wrote.

"Are you all right?" the clerk asked, staring down at her trembling hands.

Not trusting her voice, Eva simply nodded. She turned and quickly opened the door, eager to be gone before the older clerk returned. In her hurry, she stumbled over the threshold and was caught by the hands of strangers.

The street was hot and damp, and as she pushed through the crowd, it felt like walking over the hide of an animal.

*From Kamehameha the Great to Kalakaua, the spirits of all of the Hawaiian kings are gathered in this room. Queen Lili'uokalani feels them standing near, wearing their beautiful cloaks and helmets made from the red and yellow feathers of the 'i'iwi and mamo, two extinct birds. They are here to keep her company.*

*She steps closer, feels the sadness of these dead kings, especially Kamehameha III, who let the foreigners buy Hawaii's land. He stands in the corner of the room, shunned by the others. It is his shame, after all, not theirs.*

*They tell her that her Bible isn't strong enough against these people who have stolen their country. Where is your spear? they ask. You have put down your spear and picked up their Bible. Where is your spear now?*

*In the dark, she moves faster and faster between these kings of Hawaii, in their cloaks of extinction.*

# Twenty-Five

Two days after Lehua returned from Molokai, Jonathan reappeared, carrying a large satchel through the back door. He glanced at Eva and nodded, setting down the bag. It was rare to see him so bold, moving about in daylight.

"This evening it would be good for you to be away from the house," he said.

"Why?"

"Why not? Go downtown. Have a good time."

"A good time," she repeated. "And are you also telling Lehua what she should do?"

"Lehua isn't here. She's visiting friends on the windward side, and should be gone for several days."

"She's gone? She's just come home." Eva took hold of his arm. "What are you planning?"

He shook his head.

"Why won't you talk to me? What can you yourself do against an entire government?"

"Miss Hanson," he said flatly, "you have been helpful. But now it is time for you to mind your own affairs, not mine."

She pulled back. His voice was so cold, he might have slapped her.

He read her expression and began to say something, then changed his mind and was silent.

"I am trying to understand, but you make it impossible."

"There is nothing to understand. You must stay with your own kind."

Eva flushed at his remark. "What kind would that be?"

"Haole."

Furious, she ran upstairs to her room and locked the door. He's wrong, she thought. Some people have no kind.

A moment later, she heard him come up the stairs. The storeroom door opened and then locked shut, and she heard him going back downstairs.

Yes, she thought, I will leave. Better than sitting here listening all night.

She opened the wardrobe and took out her jacket. There was a small wrapped package in the pocket. She unfolded the brown paper. It was Lehua's tortoiseshell comb, one of the few belongings of her mother's that she still owned. Eva held it in her hand, wondering. Then she brushed back her hair and set the comb in, exactly as Lehua wore it. She turned and looked in the mirror. It was like a hand cupping the back of her head.

She took it off and wrapped it back up in the paper and put it in the suitcase, next to her tarot cards. She pulled on the jacket and stepped into the hall. Jonathan had left a small metal bowl of fruit just outside her door. She kicked it out of the way, sending the bowl spinning across the hall.

$\mathcal{A}$t night, the sound of the ocean became more insistent, the give and take between land and sea more obvious. Downtown, the streets were full of Americans. More than a week had passed since Queen Lili'uokalani's imprisonment, and most of the Royalists had been captured. The government lifted the curfew, but only the Americans were secure enough to believe it. Everyone else expected more trouble. At dusk, the Hawaiians and Chinese hurried home, while the Japanese disappeared behind sliding shoji doors.

That afternoon, Cornelius Rhodes had filed the last of his land purchase deeds and was finally the owner of one of the largest land parcels on Oahu. Now he walked through town feeling that everything and everyone belonged to him: from the stacks of drygoods to the lei sellers, from the smoke of dying fires to the old woman carrying a can of black paint, he felt all of it becoming his.

*E*va had convinced McClelland to go out to dinner, and now they walked hand in hand down a street filled with the scent of plumeria and smoke, and below that the low tide smell of urine and mud. In the dark, anything could be hidden: a limp, a mouthful of rotten teeth, the beginning signs of leprosy. A land deal, a murder.

They ate dinner in a Chinese restaurant. Inside, it was too loud, and they gave up trying to talk to each other. Eva was anxious, but McClelland didn't question her, just watched her carefully. She was glad for the noises coming from the kitchen, the clatter of cooking pots, the Chinese voices sharp as knives.

She thought of Jonathan and nervously touched the netsuke rabbit on the cord around her neck. Is it any wonder that I am praying for luck, she thought, now that there isn't any left.

She wondered if whatever Jonathan had planned had already taken place. How would she know when it was safe to go home?

McClelland pointed out that she hadn't eaten anything, so Eva took a few bites of each dish, feigning interest.

He smiled at her efforts. "You are preoccupied tonight."

"Yes, I am," she agreed, not trusting herself to say anything further.

Through the window, they watched off-duty soldiers and haole businessmen gathered in small damp groups. Colored lanterns dangled over club entrances, and brightly dressed women fluttered like moths around the lights.

"You don't really want to be here, do you? I mean, in this restaurant."

She shook her head.

He set his chopsticks down and suggested that they leave.

Outside the restaurant, a boy in a pair of ragged shorts wove through the crowd. A merchant chased after him, hindered by a long apron double wrapped around his thick belly. After the boy flashed past, Eva stepped out into the path of the merchant. He slowed down to avoid running into her, and the boy melted into the darkness.

Eva nervously linked her arm through McClelland's.

Tonight, everything seemed temporary. Music leaked out of the bars only to evaporate in the air. In the frenzy of buying drinks and exchanging greetings, there was a feeling that nothing could be held onto. Not friendship, or money, or loyalty. In the shadows, couples wound together out of desperation as much as lust, afraid that if they let go of each other they'd disappear.

A crowd was gathered around the butcher shop, pointing at the windows splattered with black paint. Small targets, Eva thought.

A carriage stopped next to them, and a wide brimmed hat leaned out of the window. The face under it asked McClelland directions to the Columbia Club.

He shook his head. "I've never heard of it."

"That's odd. I was told it was on this street."

"Sorry." McClelland gave Eva's elbow a warning squeeze.

"Be careful," he murmured as they crossed to the other side of the street and moved quickly through the crowd.

They stopped to buy meat sticks from a woman busy cooking over a heated brazier. A hand reached forward and grabbed hold of Eva's arm. She turned and stabbed whoever it was with the end of the bamboo skewer. He yelled and dropped his hand.

Someone else knocked McClelland backwards into a wall, and as he struggled, they both slipped into the mud.

Eva was dragged down the street, with her head pushed down and fingers digging into her skin. All she could see were hard black shoes.

She quit struggling and pulled a faint her mother would have been proud of. As she collapsed to the ground, the fingers loosened and then let go.

McClelland was yelling something, but she couldn't make it out, she was kicking away from the black shoes, her hands full of mud as she scrambled across the road.

Then she heard what McClelland was yelling. Run.

She was on her feet, running with no thought of direction, running wildly through the damp crowd that made way for her. She ran past the clubs and a line of people waiting to buy lottery tickets, and then down a small road with a row of wooden shacks. She raced through an overgrown lot, branches whipping against her face and arms until finally she crouched down against the back wall of a cottage, trying to catch her ragged breath, which seemed to be coming from somewhere outside her body.

Next door, a lantern moved from the front of the cottage towards the back, and then a door opened onto the back lanai. A woman swung the lantern out across the yard, giving her a clear view of Eva crouched against the wall.

Please don't say a word, Eva thought, but the woman was already screaming. She yelled the color of Eva's hair—not ehu, which was red for Hawaiian hair, but po'o 'ula'ula, which was red for haole hair.

Eva leapt up and ran. Behind her, the woman continued to scream. She scrambled over a fence, felt her skirt catch and rip. Then a hand grabbed hold of her wrist and twisted and she fell to the ground.

A man crouching over her yelled, "We've got her."

She was shoved into a carriage, landing on her hands and knees, with her face pushed down into the seat. Think of them as dogs, she told herself, willing herself to stop trembling, to turn her fear into something she could manage.

Her hair was pulled and her neck snapped back. She looked up, expecting to see Rhodes, but it was someone else.

"You've some explaining to do."

She scrambled up off the floor and sat down in the opposite seat.

The man leaned forward and smiled at her with small perfect teeth the size of an infant's. "To the jail," he told the driver, then blew out the small lamp that hung against the door.

In the dark carriage, Eva asked what she was being charged with, as if it mattered. As if anyone in Honolulu followed the rule of law.

He didn't answer.


$\mathcal{T}$he street in front of the jail was clogged with wagons and carts and people holding up money, attempting to buy the freedom of jailed relatives. Men carrying lanterns yelled contradictory instructions that were ignored by everyone.

Eva was shoved through the crowd and into the jail. She had been to jail before, but this was not like debtor's prison. Debtors' prison had a resigned smell, like old dirt. This jail smelled of fear as sharp as drying seaweed. The scent made her stomach churn.

There was no one behind the desk, no one to take down her name. She was pushed through a narrow hallway and put in a cell without a window. The heat quickly became unbearable, and within minutes her clothing was drenched.

Her thoughts jumped in all directions at once. She pushed her forehead against the wall and stood like that for a long time, turning over everything she knew, everything that had happened. She still came up emptyhanded.

No one came to question her. The hours passed. She took off her blouse and wrung it out, then put it on again.

She was left alone overnight. The next morning, the cell door opened and a crowd of young Hawaiian women spilled through the doorway. Eva was glad for the company.

They had the resigned air of those who've been to jail many times. One of the women had brought her knitting, and as the day turned hot and sticky, the only sound was the insectlike clicking of the needles.

Eva stretched out on a bench, closed her eyes, and felt the women watching her. What was she to them, with her freckled skin and her bright red hair? An anomaly. Haole women didn't go to jail. Haole women had enough money to stay out of trouble.

After several hours, one of the women asked Eva why she was being held.

Was there any reason to tell the truth? That she'd found the body of a man who wasn't ever supposed to be found, and now they were hounding her for it.

Eva sat up. "I was making pills," she answered. "Selling them as cures for various ailments."

In a shy voice the woman asked if the pills worked.

"No, not really. They were just sugar."

The woman spoke to the others in Hawaiian, and they all laughed. Eva laughed as well, surprised by her own honesty.

"Kilokilo?" another woman asked.

Eva answered yes, she was a fortuneteller and she offered to read palms, but no one was interested in the future.

They explained that they usually spent two days in jail and then the man they worked for came with bail. "It happens when the police need money," the knitter explained. "Waihine ho'oka-makama," she said.

Prostitutes. Eva thought of her mother, who had spent many nights in jail, finally bailed out by one lover or another. But not always. There were nights when she was left there, as these women were now.

In the middle of the night, a guard woke Eva by hitting the bottom of her feet with a stick.

She joined a small crowd of exhausted people, and they were herded down a different hallway and into a large room already full of people, some of whom looked like they'd been there for weeks.

The lanterns were taken away, and they were left in darkness.

Eva found a wall and crouched down against it. Her hair was damp with sweat, her arm beginning to swell where the man's fingernails had broken the skin.

A story circulated that a man had tried to break into the palace and free the Queen. He'd wounded six government soldiers before he was shot.

Eva hoped it wasn't Jonathan.

If anyone moved, they moved quietly, stood up and stretched, then sat down again. Eva lost all sense of time, not knowing whether she had been in the room for five hours or twenty.

A guard called out a name. A thin man in ragged clothes stood up and was led out of the room. A moment later, there was the sound of wood on flesh, and a low groaning. When he didn't come back, someone began singing softly, a song written by Queen Lili'uokalani, and the rest of the room joined in.

The side of Eva's mouth twitched. She pushed her hand against her face, unable to stop her mouth from moving. She wondered what death felt like. Not dying, dying was horrible, dying was about being in rooms like this. No, she was thinking of death itself. Tomas always claimed that death was nothing more than the weight of a rooster on an old man's chest.

She told herself that McClelland had escaped, that he was now safe. It was unbearable to think otherwise. She pulled her knees to her chest, trying to make herself smaller.

To sit and wait for what would come next was both terrifying and monotonous. The hours went by in drips, in breaths. They were not allowed to go to the bathroom. Instead, they used buckets in the corner of the room. "You natives," a guard said, "should be used to this."

After the guard left, there was the faint sound of a stick running across the small barred window at the end of the room. Small pieces of pipi kaula were quickly slipped through the bars. Eva chewed on a piece of dried beef the size of a silver dollar and was soon racked with thirst.

People talked in tired undertones. No one mentioned food or water. The best way to deal with hunger was to sleep through it.

That evening, a whispered message was passed down the row of people huddled against the wall. Eva was told to go to the window.

In the dark, she stepped carefully over arms and legs, and by the time she got to the window no one was there. On the outer windowsill there was a small flower, too far away for her fingers to reach. She held onto the bars, straining to hear McClelland's voice, but it was just a Kona wind, blowing everything in the opposite direction. Her grandmother called a wind like that a bride running backwards.

As she moved back through the crowd, hands reached up and brushed against her skirt. When she sat down again, the old man next to her patted her shoulder, and she thought that to be comforted at that moment only made her realize the extent of her distress.

When she could speak, she asked the old man what the charge against him was.

"Treason," he said, "like everyone else."

He sounded far younger than he appeared, in the way that grief and poverty erode a face faster than age.

He told her his name was Malo.

"Liv," she said. "I am Liv Norseng." It was a relief to finally tell someone her name.

Malo nodded and gently touched her arm. "Sleep now," he whispered, and she did.

*Uwe ka lani, ola ka honua: the heavens weep, the land lives. And yet what happens to heaven if the land is weeping?*

# Twenty-Six

$E$va slept with her head on Malo's shoulder, and when she woke up she was surprised to find a young boy curled up next to her. She gave Malo a questioning glance.

He rubbed his shoulder and whispered that the boy must be missing his mother. When the child woke, Malo questioned him, but he refused to speak.

Eva noticed him staring at the netsuke rabbit. She took it off and gave it to him to play with, wondering how someone so young could be in jail.

When he finally spoke, it was to ask Eva if her red hair was real.

Eva nodded and pulled the comb out of her hair and shook it loose. The boy told her that there was another color of red which was called 'ohi'a 'ai, a birthmark caused when a pregnant mother longed for mountain apples.

Eva thought of Rhodes's red face, and wondered what his mother had longed for when she was pregnant with him. A great slab of beef, she decided.

"Why are you here?" she asked.

"To help my Queen," the boy answered shyly.

"That's good," she said, and took hold of his hand and squeezed it.

He let the red haired woman hold his hand until she fell back asleep, then he gently pried her fingers loose and shook his hand until the feeling came back.

A storm woke Eva, fists of rain that pounded the tin roof of the jail. Men stood at the window, pushing their fingers through the bars to catch a little rainwater. Eva turned to ask the boy if he was thirsty, but he wasn't there.

"Taken away during the night," Malo said.

"By who?" Eva asked. "The soldiers?"

Malo shook his head, not answering.

"By who?" she repeated.

"By death."

"How can that be?" she whispered softly.

He said that the boy was wounded but didn't tell anyone. He must have thought he was helping by not saying anything. "I don't even know his name," he added.

He handed Eva her necklace and she bit the inside of her mouth to keep from crying. In Hawaiian, heart was pu'uwai, she told herself. In Norwegian, hjerte.

How could she not have seen that the boy was hurt, that there was something wrong?

In the middle of the night the door opened, and a man was shoved into the room. The door closed, and bolts were scraped shut. Several men crouched over him, feeling for broken bones.

Word spread that he was the last of the Royalists who'd been up in the mountains, sabotaging the Americans. Malo shook his head, said it was impossible for a handful of men to hold off the Republic's soldiers.

A hero, Eva thought.

The wounded man demanded light and food, and for some reason the guards complied. A lantern was brought into the room, and Eva and Malo looked quickly away from each other, the bright light making them suddenly shy.

When the guards brought in fish and poi, a few of the men in the room began to weep softly.

The wounded man was moved to their side of the room, and Malo touched his arm. "Sorry you are in so much trouble," he said softly.

The man shrugged. "I am always in trouble."

Eva asked Malo if he had heard about the dead man that the papers reported found in the canal down in Waikiki.

He nodded.

She told him the true story, that she had found him on the beach and that he had been murdered for his land.

"Kalama was a farmer up in Nuuanu Valley. His wife didn't even know she was a widow."

He told Eva that as soon as she was released from jail she should go to the newspapers with the true story, but they were of the same mind, wondering what good it would do. The editors of the Hawaiian newspapers were themselves in jail, and the only papers still allowed to publish were those favorable to the Republic of Hawaii.

Later that night, a guard called Eva Hanson's name.

Malo squeezed her hand and she slowly stood up. She was momentarily confused, thinking that now she would be taken to identify the boy whose name no one knew.

Instead, she was taken across the hall, into another room that smelled of wet dirt and urine.

A large man followed her into the room and locked the door behind him.

She couldn't stop her legs from shaking.

"Why did you come to Hawaii?" he asked.

Because I was running away. Because I didn't want to go to jail in Norway, she thought. Not knowing that I would end up in a jail here.

*The Floating City* · 253

She gave him the only answer he'd believe. "For the money."

"I thought so," he said, disgustedly.

"Ah. So your presence on this island is a much higher calling, then," she said.

He didn't answer. Instead, he turned and left the room, taking her temporary bravado with him.

She was afraid to move, fearful of what she might find, but eventually she felt her way along the wall, slowly kicking at the darkness in front of her. There was nothing in the room except a tin bucket for waste. She turned it over and sat down on it.

She had no idea what would happen next. Perhaps they would keep her there, in that room. Perhaps they had already forgotten about her.

After a long time, she thought to thump on the side wall. No one answered back.

It was much worse being alone.

The hours passed. Then McClelland was suddenly there in the room with her, she was certain that she felt the pressure of his hand against the small of her back, and then just as quickly he was gone, and she was left with an unbearable sadness.

Footsteps came down the hall, and a nearby door was opened. A moment later, there was the sickening sound of wood hitting flesh. Eva crawled into the corner farthest from the door and pressed her palms against her ears.

Later, she woke up to a rectangle of light, and hands that reached under her arms and pulled her to her feet. Her body was numb, and her legs didn't seem to be working. She was dragged out of the cell and down a hall. She couldn't see anything at all except the same rectangle of light, seared onto her eyes.

She was shoved into a bright room and told to wait. She closed her eyes against the light, put her hands out the same way she had done in the darkness, and when she touched the edge of a chair she sat down.

This isn't happening to me, she told herself, it is happening to Eva Hanson.

Someone entered the room, and she turned in that direction. Her eyes were watering and she couldn't see much, just the dark shape of a man.

"Eva."

It was Edward. She sobbed in relief.

"My God, are you all right?" He held her until she stopped crying, then pulled a handkerchief from his pocket and wiped off her face.

"How did you know I was here?"

"Believe me, I wish I didn't. The Widow and Tomas contacted me. They've been trying to get you out for days, but they're not letting anyone but haoles near the jail. You would not believe the amount of money it's cost me just to get this far." He opened his briefcase on the table and pulled out a thick pile of papers.

Edward was unpredictable. That much hadn't changed. "Where is McClelland?" she asked.

Edward ignored her question.

"I was running away, he told me to run. . . . Edward, I need to get a message to him."

"He's disappeared."

"They've taken him prisoner?"

"No, I mean actually disappeared. There are many rumors floating about, but the one that seems most credible is that he and another man took a boat to Maui. A brother or something."

Eva was relieved. "Thank God," she said.

"He'd better stay there, too. There's a warrant for his arrest. You know how to pick them, Eva."

He glanced nervously through his papers, not bothering to read anything. "Listen," he said, then stopped.

She didn't like the tone of his voice, didn't like what he was going to say next. She chewed the inside of her mouth, waiting.

"I'm here to get you out."

"I am held illegally."

"No, you're not. Do you have any idea what they are charging you with?"

"Treason."

He waved a hand in dismissal. "Everyone is being charged with that. This is much worse. A murder charge. They're accusing you of murdering the man you found on the beach."

"That is ridiculous."

"Eva, look around. Hasn't it occurred to you that these people get what they want?"

And that's why you are with them, she thought. You've gone over to their side. "This is about Rhodes, isn't it?"

Edward lowered his voice. "You don't understand, do you? It's much bigger than Rhodes. He was working for important people, and he made some mistakes."

Yes, she thought. He killed Kalama and then signed his name as the buyer of that man's property. They must have been so pleased when they saw me coming. A perfect scapegoat. A woman of dubious reputation with a connection to a dead man.

"Rhodes is the kind of man to distance yourself from," he added.

"What about you, Edward. Have you distanced yourself from him?"

He opened his hands and smiled. "Barely knew the man."

Eva shook her head.

"You could plead self-defense, say that the man attacked you and you were forced to kill him. But you'd still get a jail term, probably fifteen years."

Fifteen years. That was impossible. "They can't prove it."

"Come, now. You're a fortuneteller. Who's going to defend you? You're not even American. No one will believe your side of it, because no one cares."

He stood up and paced the length of the room. "It gets worse."

"How can it possibly get worse?"

"Eva, they went through your house. You know what they found upstairs? Gunpowder, fuses. Everything you need to make bombs. A lot of it, too."

She saw Jonathan, carrying the satchel. So he has failed as well, she thought, not knowing if she was disappointed or relieved. "It wasn't mine," she whispered.

"No. I know it wasn't yours. You have many talents, but even this government can figure out that building bombs isn't one of them."

She looked at him. "What, then?"

"They want a name."

"I don't have a name."

"Eva, don't be ridiculous."

"So, if I give them a name, can I stay here?"

"Only if you're in jail."

"Then why should I give them anything?"

"To clear yourself. Look at this realistically. Your choices are jail or exile."

Exile.

"You leave this country, promise never to come back. It will be listed as an unsolved crime."

He pushed a piece of paper into her hands. "They want the matter closed. All you have to do is sign."

She stared at the paper without reading it.

"You don't have to be heroic."

She shook her head. "There isn't anything heroic about it."

"All right. Bullheadedness, if you like. Just sign the paper, Eva."

"Are you being paid for this?"

He ignored the question. "Believe me, it's lucky that you are well known in this town. It's the only thing that's kept you safe. You have no idea what these people are capable of."

Eva tried to keep her voice calm. "If this is to remain an unsolved crime, then why do I have to sign a confession?"

"As insurance."

"But what if I went to Maui instead?"

"You can't do that. They want you to leave the country."

"So if I ever came back here . . ."

"But you won't. This place is used up for you."

"No," she said. "It isn't."

He stared at her a moment and shook his head. "Ah, Eva. I never thought you were the type to fall in love."

She didn't answer.

He shrugged. "A few more years and I'll probably be escorted out of here myself. Listen, if you tried to come back and they caught you, who knows what they'd do to you in jail."

Eva looked down at her hands, the nails broken and caked with mud. She had seen the end coming and tried to ignore it. The life you chose is the one that gets away from you.

She picked up the pen and signed Eva Hanson's name at the bottom of a page where she confessed to having murdered Mr. Kalama in a fit of passion.

"I'm not going back to Europe," she said in a low voice.

"No, I knew you wouldn't want that. I've got you a ticket to San Francisco."

She looked up. San Francisco? It was rumored to be a gold rush of pocket watches and jewelry, bachelors with sackfuls of gold nuggets and nowhere near enough pickpockets. And McClelland all the way across the ocean.

"There is a ticket held for you at the harbormaster's office."

A guard knocked at the door and opened it. "Time," he said.

They stood up. Eva turned back down the hall, towards a slumped over man with blood pouring down his face.

"No," the guard said, "the other way."

Edward spoke to the guard for a moment. The guard nodded and unlocked the door. Edward leaned forward and kissed her cheek. "Here's some money."

"Whose money?"

He smiled and shook his head. "Does it matter? Pay me back when you can. You've only a short time to settle your affairs. And listen," he added, "they're still keeping an eye on you. Be careful where you take them."

She walked out of the jail and onto the street.

There is coral under this street, she thought, and waves are rushing through it, and still people live their lives as if this were solid ground. As if tomorrow were guaranteed.

In front of the jail, a crowd was gathered around a missionary perched on a little black box. He held up his Bible and shook it like a tambourine, and Eva thought that in the mouths of some men, even God was someone's pet monkey.

She looked through the crowd, hoping to find Lehua or Mc-Clelland waiting for her, but of course they weren't. Her skirt was torn and her boots were caked with mud that fell off in clumps as she slowly walked through Honolulu. The heat was record breaking, the kind of heat that turned people mindless, that buckled the legs faster than strong drink. Fans blurred in the hands of people with shining wet faces, and the dogs flattened themselves into the dirt. Eva turned up the long road to Lehua's house.

There wasn't much time, and still she couldn't make herself walk any faster, her legs slow as syrup poured from a jar.

She didn't care about packing her clothing. All she wanted was a tortoiseshell comb, a glass ball, and her grandmother's tarot cards.

She thought of one of Mormor's jokes. How do you know if you are still alive?

If everything is still unbearable.

She paused under a fire-colored poinsettia tree and leaned

her forehead against the trunk, closing her eyes against the future.

The dock would be crowded with people and baggage, and lei sellers offering orchids and plumerias and pikake, but none would be as beautiful as the lei the Widow would have made for her if there had been time.

At the edge of the pier, the brass band would play the kind of music that played as the pubs closed, the boats left, the body was lowered into the ground. Tomas would weep the dry tears of an old man, and everyone would pretend that Eva would come back, once this war was over, and the Americans were gone for good.

A journey taken over water is better than one taken over land, she reminded herself. A river is better than a road, and the ocean is the best yet.

It would be impossible to say goodbye to these people she'd had to come halfway around the world to meet. What was the point of it? There was no sense in finding out how many pieces you could break yourself into. Instead, she'd leave the way she arrived, without notice, carrying a small suitcase and a dead woman's name.

She pushed through the damp crowd, waiting for someone to see that everything in her life had changed. But this was just another day to them, a day filled with heat and soldiers.

# Epilogue

$E$va didn't stay long in San Francisco. It was true that the people were careless with their wealth, spending their gold as quickly as they found it, but she had become used to trade winds wrapping round her like a warm shawl, and the city was too cold, too much like Norway.

Journeying south along a coastline where the Pacific Ocean spent itself over the rocks, she stared out at the sea, not looking in the direction of Hawaii, just watching the water gather and spend itself. Her thoughts were bits of paper blowing away before she could catch hold of them.

She traveled constantly, attempting to keep grief away through motion. She moved through small villages, telling fortunes and finding that she was as scared of the future as anyone else, now treating it as carefully as a door opening onto a roomful of fire.

There were dry lands full of cactus and bleached bones of cattle, and towns that froze at night and melted during the day. When strangers came through town, they were directed to the Norwegian fortuneteller, and Eva was good at knowing what strangers wanted to hear. After all, she was one herself.

In the plaza of a small village, Eva watched as a woman leaned forward over a fountain while a friend quickly poured a pitcher of water across the nape of her neck. She flung her wet hair backwards, laughing as it flew over her head and slapped down against her back like a dark wave.

The streets were full of dogs as thin as paper, and although she knew that the wealth of a town could be told by the weight of its animals, she decided to stop there. Each morning she opened the window of her boardinghouse to listen to the women washing their clothes in the center of town.

One night, in a small restaurant the size of a kitchen, Eva felt someone watching her. When she looked up, the dead man Kalama was standing in the open doorway. She closed her eyes, steadied herself against the edge of the table, then looked again. There he was. Unbidden. He nodded when he caught her eye, and then he passed through the warped glass of a window and disappeared.

When she returned to her boardinghouse that night, she took a pen and a bottle of ink, and began a letter to Lehua. In it she said: In this town the dogs are thin as paper, but the women have hair as dark as yours. . . .